THE SAGA OF DESPAIR AND HOPE
BOOK 1

OASIS 2064

TAMAR BEN-UR

BALBOA
PRESS
A DIVISION OF HAY HOUSE

Balboa Press books may be ordered through booksellers or by contacting:

Balboa Press
A Division of Hay House
1663 Liberty Drive
Bloomington, IN 47403
www.balboapress.com
1 (877) 407-4847

Because of the dynamic nature of the Internet, any web addresses or
links contained in this book may have changed since publication and
may no longer be valid. The views expressed in this work are solely those
of the author and do not necessarily reflect the views of the publisher,
and the publisher hereby disclaims any responsibility for them.

This is a work of fiction. All the characters, organizations,
and events portrayed in this novel are either products of
the author's imagination or are used fictitiously.

The author of this book does not dispense medical advice or prescribe
the use of any technique as a form of treatment for physical, emotional,
spiritual, or medical problems without the advice of a physician, either
directly or indirectly. In the event you use any of the information in
this book for yourself, which is your constitutional right, the author
and the publisher assume no responsibility for your actions.

Certain stock imagery © Getty Images.

Print information available on the last page.

ISBN: 978-1-5043-9855-8 (sc)
ISBN: 978-1-5043-9857-2 (hc)
ISBN: 978-1-5043-9856-5 (e)

Library of Congress Control Number: 2018902338

Balboa Press rev. date: 03/27/2018

To my beloved granddaughters Maia and Dalia.

CONTENTS

PROLOGUE

In the 2,064th year of the current era, many people felt as if the world had come to an end, or at least the world as they'd known it had. Nature awoke and demonstrated its invincible power, as if to declare that it would endure no more exploitation and abuse. It was as if Mother Earth had finally decided to punish her tormentors and abusers, who, following their greed and insatiable pursuit of power, had threatened to destroy her beauty and inherent nurturing nature and to turn her into a barren, poisonous no-man's-land.

Earth rose in a fury of erupting volcanoes and earthquakes. Not only did active volcanoes and dormant ones alike spew their lava, but also mountains that had never been known as volcanic started rumbling. The earth had been shaking unexpectedly, frequently where humans had dug deep into the ground to retrieve oil or minerals. It seemed that the equilibrium that had maintained the magma, dormant under the earth's crust, was destroyed abruptly, and it was pushed out as an expression of the earth's wrath and frustration.

The elements acted synergistically to increase the disasters. Earthquakes created tsunamis and wildfires, whose energy was augmented by the powerful winds. The lava that spewed out into the oceans raised the water temperature, which resulted in hurricanes, tornadoes, severe storms, and floods. The oceans' water level rose and covered small islands and metropolises alike.

In the United States, forty million people were killed directly as a result of these disasters, and sixty million died subsequently from starvation and diseases. The rest of the world did not fare much better. Cities and villages were in shambles, and the roads were full of refugees who were willing to give everything they had for safe shelter and a secure means of subsistence.

Social institutions collapsed. Governments were incapacitated and could not ensure the supply of food and clean water to the survivors. The health and welfare systems were incapable of helping the sick and the destitute, and many were left to die. The catastrophes brought out the best and worst in people. Many opened their homes and religious temples to provide shelter to the uprooted, but others armed themselves to the teeth and robbed what little the unfortunates had.

Unsurprisingly, there was no lack of self-proclaimed prophets eager to preach and frighten these unfortunates, as if the later had not been through hell already. Religious fanatics told the people that the destruction was the result of their transgressions, while environmental zealots reminded all how they had tried to dissuade governments and corporations from polluting the atmosphere, poisoning the food supply, and depleting the soil, and how fiercely they had fought against the use of GMOs and poisonous pesticides and herbicides. Some people followed these zealots for lack of better options, especially if the preachers promised food, shelter, and employment.

Many of the CEOs of companies that were responsible for pumping carbon dioxide into the air, or obstructing legislative attempts to halt climate change, left the country as soon as they sensed fingers pointing toward them. Hefty bank accounts in foreign countries guaranteed a safe restart. These people were never prosecuted or punished. Others, however, stayed and used their power to subjugate people so as to increase their own control and wealth and create a secure and luxurious life for themselves and their loved ones, hidden from the public eye. Being known before by conspiracy theory believers as the Illuminati, they emerged after the disasters as the Order Defenders (OD). Since many of them had contributed directly or indirectly to the disasters, they governed through surrogates, using their massive amounts of capital and their private army of loyal, well-paid, and professionally trained mercenaries equipped with state-of-the-art weaponry. They emerged in the eastern United States, known west of the Mississippi as East, and threatened to broaden their control to include the rest of the country, which reorganized as Central and West.

The world was yearning for a new direction but did not seem to evolve above and beyond self-aggrandizing greed, power, and lust. Those who did evolve and who had expected other people to learn from their experience were horrified to witness how little people had changed. It seemed that greed and ignorance were humanity's everlasting incurable diseases that in the best of times had been in remission.

Some people, however, disillusioned by governments and corporations, and believing in imminent catastrophes—natural, social, or both—organized themselves into sustainable communities that provided most of the food and energy they needed. Some were driven by fear and armed themselves to defend against potential enemies. Others attempted to develop communities based on sharing and love.

The first book in this series chronicles the events occurring in the divided country from the vantage point of James Callahan, a sustainable community developer whose fate carries him across the country to experience life as an OD supporter and as a man who fights against them. This is not a story of David and Goliath or of Hercules fighting the Hydra. The modern monster has too many regenerating heads beyond one legendary hero's ability to decapitate. It takes a collaborative effort of many people, each contributing his or her personal talents and being willing to risk it all. Against this backdrop, the story highlights one community, Oasis, as a beacon of light, and follows its residents' transformation as they attempt to fight the monster.

CHAPTER 1

BACK TO OASIS

Dr. Steve Grisham drove his SUV back to Oasis, with Charlotte slumbering by his side. He was glad she was coming back with him in spite of the fact that she had foolishly betrayed him with the farmer next door and then run away to Sanctuary after the farmer started abusing her. The memory of her long, dark, curly hair and her voluptuous body had pursued him during the days and kept him awake at nights. There was nothing he wanted more than to hold her in his arms. That was why he'd hurried to Sanctuary after she had called and begged him to take her back, without thinking or asking too many questions. Now that she was within reach, he was not quite sure what he really wanted. He had the chilling feeling that he would never be able to trust her again.

Being in Sanctuary for only a few hours and experiencing the suspicious, unfriendly looks on people's faces had made him so nervous that he was relieved to leave Sanctuary behind. He had not felt safe there, to say the least. He could easily believe that Charlotte had been threatened by the notorious Jim. *No wonder Charlotte tried anything to get out of there,* he thought. *But was I her last resort? She could have probably seduced somebody in Sanctuary to take her in. Or maybe she did and got in trouble again?*

Steve's mood was gloomy. Going to Sanctuary, he'd fantasized being the hero who rescued his lover from the dragon, but now he felt more like the fallback guy who was being taken advantage of. As creative and capable as he was as a physician, he knew that as far as women were concerned, he was a novice and could be fooled easily. Approaching the age of forty, he had never had a serious relationship with a woman before Charlotte. The figure that reflected from his mirror was not unattractive, although more exercise would have been helpful. Tall, nicely built, and having thick dark hair and blue eyes, he knew that his real problem was not his looks but his being always busy with his work and research, and his lack of interest in anything beyond it. *I am the utmost nerd,* he thought, *especially with this black-framed pair of eyeglasses.* Sometimes he envied his popular colleagues who knew how to joke with nurses and clients, while he could not engage in small talk. Indeed, all he could talk about was his plants and health issues. *I am the utmost antisocial guy,* he thought, remembering how awkward he had felt at the few parties he'd agreed to attend.

So when Charlotte approached him, about half a year ago, he'd counted his blessings. She was an attractive woman, a good nurse, and a very organized and seasoned cook—what more could he desire? Finally, he could come home and have somebody waiting for him. She even put up with his endless descriptions of his research. He had thought about proposing. But his joy was short-lived. She left about three months after she'd moved in. Now he would trade all her virtues for only one: trustworthiness. He wanted his woman to stick with him and support him on rainy days. Charlotte had told him that she was sorry and that she would never let the same thing happen again, but could he trust her? Did she really care for him if she could fall for that stupid farmer? How could he be sure that she would not fall into the arms of some guy in the hospital, like the arrogant new doctor Andy, as soon as she had a chance? He smiled bitterly, thinking that none of the beautiful poisonous mushrooms he had studied and analyzed could have fooled him to consume them but that probably every woman could.

Steve tried to brush away the thoughts about Charlotte, thinking about his medical practice, the home he'd worked so hard to pay for, and his beloved greenhouse to which he could not wait to return. For a moment, it made him smile as warm feelings engulfed him. But then nagging thoughts traversed his mind. He considered Oasis his refuge from the impending calamity that everybody was talking about, knowing that in spite of the horrific disasters two years earlier, there were still more to come. He wondered if Oasis residents would stick together and help each other when another natural disaster hit. His visit to Sanctuary had convinced him that its residents would not.

He had worked so hard to pay back his student loans and to meet the nearly impossible financial conditions of Sustainable Community Developers (SCD), the company that built Oasis, and therefore he did not have time for socializing, even if he'd had the proclivity to do so. And he could not remember his last period of free time. Assuming that the others were in the same situation, and that they probably were not ready for any collective activity either, he'd accepted it as reality. But all of a sudden, he realized that this state of affairs was perilous and that getting to know each other should become the priority of Oasis residents. But how could he make it happen?

A pothole in the road jolted the car, waking Charlotte, who was visibly shaken.

"What was it?" she asked.

"Just a pothole. They don't fix the roads nowadays."

Somber, Steve continued driving, aware that they'd hardly spoken a word since he'd picked her up at Sanctuary. Finally, he uttered, "Glad to have you back, Charlotte. I missed you so much at home and in my practice. But I am not sure how much I can trust you now. I suggest that you stay in the guest room until we figure out where we are heading."

He saw her biting her lip, but he continued driving in silence.

Finally, he was elated to see Oasis in the distance. He accelerated the car. As they entered the beloved twelve-family community with its small white one-story homes surrounded by greenhouses and greenery, he slowed the car and pressed the garage opener button.

The garage door shrieked. They were at home. Steve helped Charlotte unpack her belongings and place them in the guest room. He noticed that she entered the kitchen and opened the fridge. *She is trying to go back to where we started,* he thought. *I wonder if I should give it a try.*

"I am going to see how my greenhouse is doing!" hollered Steve from the end of the corridor.

Not long after, the village alarm went off and they were both startled. "Not again!" said Steve, running to the living room, dirty from his garden work. He remembered with dread the two weeks of torrential rain, floods, earthquakes, tornadoes, and severe storms that had kept everyone at home and had ended with millions of people dead across the country and beyond.

Steve turned the communication device to the Oasis Channel, the community channel that enabled Rudolph "the Weather Man" to alert residents of adverse weather or any other possible danger, to broadcast news, and to inform the people of important events. The local network also provided video conferencing so Oasis's twelve families could communicate with each other.

Rudolph's grim face appeared on the screen. "We are expecting another storm soon. Use the safety protocol and take the needed precautions. I hope to know more by tomorrow morning. We will have a teleconference meeting tomorrow at 9:00 a.m."

"Charlotte, I will secure the doors and windows, and you will take care of food and water," said Steve. "And if you have time, please do the laundry. I left a lot of mess."

Steve hurried to pull down the heavy shutters that protected the glass windows around the home. Then he pulled down the protective screen that surrounded the house and greenhouse. This innovative device that protected the sensitive solar panels from severe storms and tornadoes was one invention that SCD, the company that built Oasis, was very proud of.

Charlotte, in the meantime, threw all the bedding, towels, and dirty clothes she had found around the home into the washer. Then she turned on the faucets in the two bathtubs and plugged the drains for an extra supply of filtered water. Next, she prepared the ingredients for baking two loaves of bread. Using her favorite healthy recipe, she made the dough and put it in the bread machine. Finally, she started fixing dinner. *I am going to get him back,* she thought. As her casserole was cooking in the oven, she hurried to change into her flattering red dress—Steve's favorite. She thought she'd done well when she saw Steve entering the kitchen smiling.

"Wonderful smell. I can't wait to eat this bread and whatever is cooking in the oven," said Steve. Charlotte noticed from the corner of her eye that he was following her movements. She accentuated them seductively as she was working diligently in the kitchen.

"Anything I can help with?" he asked.

"Why don't you check the faucets in the bathtubs before we have an overflow? Also, we may need to use the pantry as a shelter. I hope it looks better than the last time I saw it."

Looking at the pantry when she had first moved in with Steve, Charlotte could not believe that a guy who kept his lab meticulously clean and organized would have the fortified room designated as a shelter and as a storage area for provisions for emergency situations in such a jumble. Judging from the numerous unopened boxes, she assumed that he had ordered the required items on the list provided by the Sustainability Committee and used by residents to stock their pantries according to their family size. But since the pantry was not used in ordinary time, and because she could find everything she needed in the garden, the kitchen, or the local store, it was easy to forget about it. When she used to ask Steve about it, he would answer that he was too busy and would organize the pantry the next week. Then, he'd ask her to take care of it, but she left him for the farmer before she'd had a chance to.

Steve turned off the faucets and returned to Charlotte.

"Sorry, Charlotte, the pantry looks worse than when you last saw it, since I ordered more supplies that are still in the boxes they came in. It will take many hours to organize the pantry. Let's pray that we will not need it tonight. We'll get to work on it tomorrow."

Charlotte was not surprised. She had not expected Steve to change.

"Do you even know what you have there? Have you created an inventory of all the items that you ordered?"

"Haven't had a chance to," replied Steve.

The storm caught them eating dinner. The loud thunder and howling winds rushed them to finish their tasty meal and retire to their bedrooms to get some sleep before the situation became more severe. Charlotte used the bedding she had brought with to dress the old bed in the guest room. She thought of how she could make this room more livable with the items she owned.

Although it had been about three years since he'd moved in, Steve's home was not yet fully furnished and lacked any decoration. His bedroom consisted of a beautiful dark oak queen bed, two nightstands, and a dresser he had purchased secondhand in excellent condition. The office and dining area had adequate furniture as well, but the living room had just a dingy sofa and a communication device. During the first two years in Oasis, he could hardly pay the mortgage, much less invest in fancy furniture. Later, when his reputation grew and with it his income, he used his savings to purchase rare plants and seeds for his garden, or instruments for his private lab. As a bachelor, he didn't care much about the appearance of the rooms he hardly used.

Now, he realized that Charlotte was probably not thrilled to use the old bed and desk he'd moved to the guest room after getting his new bedroom furniture, but it was too late to change it. *I hope we will have no more adventures tonight,* he thought, as he turned off the light and drifted into a deep, dreamless sleep.

Early the following morning, he jumped out of bed and the first thought to penetrate his sleepy mind was, *the storm!* He ran all over the home and through the door connecting his home to the greenhouse. Relieved to see no damage, he went to the living room and turned on the communication device to get an update. Faithfield, the nearby city where both he and Charlotte worked, had sustained a lot of damage, especially in the least affluent neighborhoods. Golden Springs, the lucrative gated community on the northwest side of town, seemed to have ridden the storm out successfully, but it was not clear to what degree the survivors of other parts of town had shelter, food, clean water, or medical assistance. The news did not specify if the hospital, university, or other public institutions were operative.

Steve entered the kitchen, where Charlotte had prepared some breakfast. He grabbed some coffee and cereal and returned to the living room, waiting to hear from Rudolph. Charlotte followed suit silently. A somber and somewhat pompous Rudolph appeared on the screen.

"Good morning, all. My board shows that all the families are in attendance except for number 10. I have just sent them a message to join. It is imperative that all of us attend the community meetings."

After a few moments' silence, Rudolph continued. "Here they are! I am glad that we are all here. The good news is that our community fared well during the storm—at least so far, as it is not over yet. There is no damage to any of our structures or sustainability systems. I have just heard from Sanctuary, and they have no damage either. The bad news is that Faithfield is a disaster area. The poor neighborhoods were ravaged by the storm and some fires. Surprisingly, there was no severe damage to Faithfield State University or the two hospitals."

Steve was relieved to hear that his community had been spared, until he heard a beep from Unit 8 indicating an open line. Vanessa's face appeared on the screen. "Good morning, all. I could not sleep all night, and I am sure that what I heard was not just the storm. I heard airplanes and bombs. Are we under attack?"

"It seems so!" was Rudolph's answer. "I received confirmation that some of the damage was caused by bombs. There is no verification of the source, but most people I talked with believe that this is the work of the Order Defenders, or OD, who seem to have taken control of the East."

There was a beep from Unit 6, followed by a seemingly angry Ralph Cole, the community banker. "It must be the Russians or the Chinese. I don't believe that the US Air Force would attack American citizens. My father served in the army. They took great pride in defending our country. They would never attack a US city."

Charlotte touched the beeper. "I am Charlotte Rousseau, staying with Dr. Steve Grisham in Unit 5. I have spent two months in Sanctuary. They all believe that the Illuminati, who are now calling themselves the Order Defenders, are taking control of the government, currently only in the East, but they have plans to broaden their authority to Central. The OD have their own army, kind of a mercenary force, whose soldiers would obey any order in exchange for the substantial wages they receive."

Steve was pale and felt overcome by terror. That's not what he'd imagined. Like many others, he expected natural disasters as a result of climate change and did everything he could to be ready. He worked ninety hours a week at three different jobs to pay for his home and greenhouse and to buy the items on the emergency list. He had foreseen himself as the benevolent doctor who shows up where needed, helping the survivors. Although he heard the rumors about the Illuminati in the East, he had never thought they would reach Oasis. A civil war—a human-created disaster—was not on his radar, and he was not prepared emotionally to deal with it. And Charlotte had not mentioned anything about it before.

Rudolph's voice brought him back to reality. "I have just received information that our governor will speak this evening around nine o'clock. I suggest that we meet tomorrow at nine in the morning to discuss the situation. We expect another wave of the storm this afternoon, so I recommend that nobody leaves the community."

"Good morning. I am Daniel from Unit 12. I am aware that we all have been busy working hard to pay bills and get ready for any potential catastrophe, and therefore we have not had the time or energy to socialize and get to know each other. Ready or not, the catastrophe is here, and we who have lived here for about three years do not know much about each other besides connecting names with faces. Maybe it is just Freda and me, but I feel that we need to meet more often, get to know each other, and decide how we are going to live together as a community. We trusted Mark and Donna to manage our water and energy supplies and communication needs, and they have done a great job. But that's not enough. We should elect a council and form committees to deal with food, education, social life ..."

"You are right, Daniel," Rudolph said, cutting him short, "but first off, we have no place to meet face-to-face. Our designated community center is an eyesore in the middle of our little village, and SCD is out for good. Unless we build it ourselves, it will never happen. Second, I agree with you that we need to know more about each other and figure out what each of us can contribute to the community before we elect people for positions. I propose to do it tomorrow online. But now we must get ready to deal with the storm. I will send messages during the day if I get some information you need to be aware of right away. Oh, by the way, Henri, you worked for Callahan building this community. Any idea what it will take to complete the community center?"

"Good morning!" Henri's smiling face showed on the screen, resting on his strong hand that was no stranger to hard work. "Yes indeed! I did work on several projects for James Callahan, Oasis included. So, I do have the plans for the community center. I also have access to some building materials locked in the basement that we can use. We will need about one hundred thousand dollars to do all the interior work and buy appliances and furniture, provided that some of the work such as the painting would be carried out by the residents. The design calls for three levels. The basement will serve as a sports area and also be for shelter and storage. Level one will have a big hall for communal meetings and meals, a nice-size kitchen, and I think seven smaller rooms that we can use as classrooms, committee meeting places, hobby workshops, or whatever. The second floor is not entirely designed. My suggestion is to turn it into two apartments, or two apartments and an efficiency, and rent or sell them. It will provide us the income that would cover some of the expenses."

"Very encouraging," replied Rudolph. "Ralph, you are our banker. Can we get the money?"

"Well, I think that if we agree that every household pays a onetime local tax of two thousand dollars and some monthly fee after that, I can arrange a loan for the remainder. But we will have to elect an officer who is responsible for the community treasury and is authorized to sign checks, make loans, purchase materials, and do more on behalf of the community. It cannot be me because of a conflict of interest. I hope there is somebody else here who knows something about handling money."

Rudolph's face reappeared on the screen. "Sounds good! Have a good day. And unless something unexpected happens, we will teleconference tomorrow morning at nine o'clock." The screen went black.

"What do we have to do to prepare for the storm that we have not done yet?" Steve was confused.

"For starters, we need to get the pantry organized," responded Charlotte. She then disappeared into the pantry. Steve was relieved and happy to go back to his garden and studies, knowing that the pantry would finally be taken care of without his having to lift a finger.

Steve firmly believed that conventional medicine was insufficient even in good times, where all the required technology was available, and where there was ample supply of drugs. He was confident that when disaster hit, the supply line of drugs and other medical supplies would be severed and holistic medicine based on locally grown herbs would provide the only available treatments. Therefore, he spent as much as time as he could studying the medical benefits of various plants, experimenting with new treatments, and making sure he had the needed seeds or plants and the knowledge of how to grow them. Luckily, he could rely upon Marcus Gilman's extensive work *Medicinal Herbs around the Globe*, published only five years ago. This excellent book, the culmination of Gilman's life research, depicted herbs and other plants used by herbalists, medicine men or women, and shamans all over the world, complete with information on how to grow, prepare, and use them. Gilman studied any manuscript he could find and went to remote areas to study with the few healers still alive. Steve was determined to continue Gilman's work by growing herbs, experimenting with his clients, and providing scientific proof of the herbs' effectiveness.

He returned to the kitchen a few hours later to get something to eat and found Charlotte, looking quite exhausted, sitting at the table and sipping an interesting-seeming drink. Looking around, his eyes fell on new items on the kitchen counter. "What are those things? Where did they come from?" he asked.

"I guess you forgot that you ordered an expensive food processor, a food dehydrator, and a variety of canning jars," she answered, trying hard not to laugh. "They were buried under cartons of food."

Steve entered the pantry. All he could say was, "Wow! No more boxes on the floor." All the items were grouped and labeled nicely on the shelves and in drawers. He could finally see the beautiful bamboo flooring. "That's wonderful, Charlotte. Thanks. I don't believe you had a chance to start the inventory yet."

"I did not," responded Charlotte, "but I can tell you that you have enough flour to bake bread for a year, plenty of grains, cereals, and crackers, and a hefty quantity of canned meats and sardines, but not a whole lot of preserves of fruits and veggies."

"But Charlotte, you forgot about the garden!" exclaimed Steve, quite insulted that she had questioned his judgment.

"Okay, but there are some nonfood items, such as cleaning materials, hygiene supplies … I will create the inventory and see what the program suggests that we buy."

Waiting for the evening, Charlotte and Steve spent the entire day doing things around the house. The communication device broadcasted long sharp beeps that made Charlotte and Steve drop what they are doing, run to the living room, and sit down, as far away from each other as possible, on the sofa. The communication device stood on a shaky table that Steve had found on the pavement in town. None of them liked this barren room. Steve had vowed time and again to save enough money for nice new furniture, but every time he had some money saved, there appeared new items on the emergency list that he needed to purchase, and more investments into the garden and his research that he believed were absolutely necessary.

Governor Adam Hickman's figure appeared on the screen. Steve could not ignore Charlotte's look of admiration when gazing at his slender, sinewy body.

"My fellow citizens! I wish I could be a messenger of good news. Unfortunately, I am going to share awful news, and I am not going to sugarcoat the situation. We all need maximum information, full transparency, and a high level of cooperation to meet the challenges we are facing. We will have to work together and help each other if we wish to save our lives and dignity.

"Yesterday we were hit by nature and acts of treason. A severe storm created havoc, in particular in the northeast part of our state. I don't have full information yet, but according to the last reports, more than one thousand people are dead, and about five thousand homes were either destroyed or severely damaged. Apparently, the damage is even more severe.

"Some of you might have heard airplanes flying over Denver and vicinity. Because of the storm, it was hard to discern the other noises, those of bombs falling on the city of Faithfield. Controllers from our nearby air force base intercepted two of the airplanes, and we asked the pilots to land in the base's field, promising full amnesty. We hit another aircraft, and the rest flew back to East. We learned that the Illuminati, a.k.a. the Order Defenders, took control of the government illegally, and have the support of some congressmen, corporations, and generals. Nobody has seen President Rockwell for at least two weeks, and there is no information about his whereabouts. So, we have no legitimate president, and our Congress is a puppet of the Illuminati.

"We also found out that the OD started out by appearing as saviors, building housing for people whose homes were destroyed by the storms and hurricanes that hit the East. This helped them to get their people into high government positions as well as the states' and federal congresses. Soon it became evident that the entire enterprise had been a scheme to virtually enslave the residents of those housing developments and help them seize control of the East. Now, the OD are trying to scare us into surrendering to them as well.

"As the highest elected officer of the free people of Colorado, I decided to sever our ties with Washington, DC. We will funnel federal taxes to the state, and our state government will carry out the duties currently performed by the federal government. We have already started planning to restructure the government departments. I salute the enthusiasm our employees are bringing to the tasks ahead. I talked with the commanders of the air force and army bases in our state, and they are all in agreement about severing any coordination with the commander in chief or Congress."

Steve jumped off the sofa and started pacing back and forth in the small living room.

"Charlotte, it cannot be happening! What our governor is telling us is that the United States of America is no more and we are on our own. So does this mean I am no longer a US citizen? It does not make sense!"

Charlotte answered softly, "Steve, would you rather be under the OD regime? I think we need to pay attention to the rest of the speech and find out what our governor's plans are."

Steve returned to the sofa. Still very upset and trying to overcome his anger and fear, he resolved to listen to the rest of the speech.

"Evidently, we cannot resist the federal government all by ourselves. The governors of Texas, New Mexico, and Oklahoma are taking similar steps, and I hope that more Central and Mountain states will join in. I offered to provide a meeting place and residence in Denver for a Coordination Council that will represent all the participating states and ensure the supply of food, energy, lodging, and safety to the population, as well as ensure the functioning of other vital services such as health, education, intelligence, transportation, and communication.

"We need to live as sustainably as possible. Each family is encouraged to grow at least some of the food required for the survival of the household and to use renewable energy as much as possible. I instructed our higher-education institutions, broadcasting stations, and local governments to coordinate this endeavor."

"We are doing it already," uttered Steve angrily, as he continued to listen in disbelief.

"We are welcoming people who defect from the East. We should help them settle in our free states. However, we know that Illuminati spies live among us. Some may come to us as refugees seeking help. We should keep our hearts open to loving our neighbors and be aware of any suspicious activity simultaneously. Under no circumstances should you take the law into your hands! Our intelligence services will thoroughly investigate every suspicion. I know that we are facing an immense task, but I am sure we will all rise to the occasion.

"God bless you and all the freedom-loving citizens of the United States of America. God bless our new coalition of the willing."

The screen of the communication device turned black. Steve was flabbergasted, realizing that being a part of a civil war was now more probable than ever.

Charlotte, noticing his bewilderment, just said, "In Sanctuary, everybody is talking about the Illuminati and mistrust of their neighbors and the village council. Everybody is suspected of being a traitor. That's one reason why it was so terrible to live there, and why I am so thankful that you came to get me out of there."

"It sounds like there were more reasons for your wish to escape Sanctuary. We should find time to talk about your Sanctuary experience. I did not ask you about it when you called because I sensed that you were in great danger, and then you slept pretty much all the way from Sanctuary to Oasis."

"We can do it right now, Steve. I am not trying to hide anything from you. I have not told you about my stay in Sanctuary because we have been too busy preparing for the storm. I left you for Bradly because he promised me a pie in the sky. I was fooled, and did not realize it until he started treating me as a maid and became violent. I heard that he is no longer here."

"Thank God, no! He left Oasis shortly after you did. And he left a lot of debts to the bank as well. And that is not all. About a month after he left, his wife showed up looking for him. Later, the farm was sold to Bill and Liz Tarver. They look like a lovely, hardworking couple raising their two teenagers. Actually, I think those are Liz's kids, not his. She lost her husband and married Bill. They make delicious dairy products."

Charlotte bit her lip. Not having known that Bradly was married, she felt even more humiliated. She continued sheepishly. "I guess I have made a lot of bad choices in my life. Bradly is only one of them. Unfortunately, escaping to Sanctuary turned out to be a repeat of the same pattern. I rented an efficiency there, hoping to get together with Dr. Wilson, whom I know from the hospital. It turned out that he could not care less about me. My reputation followed me, and no decent guy has even come close. Instead, I was threatened and harassed by Jim, a power-monger and womanizer. I would come home from work and would not dare to come out of my apartment."

For a moment she stopped talking, reminiscing about the beauty of Sanctuary, an upscale community built by SCD. The beautiful homes were bigger and had more lavish features than the Oasis homes. But the residents who were affluent enough to afford them were nothing like Oasis residents. Many had made their fortunes illegally on Wall Street or in other financial institutions and had withdrawn to Sanctuary before their schemes were discovered. No wonder they were fearful and mistrusting.

"Sanctuary is so beautiful," she continued. "And you should have seen their beautiful community center! Unlike the way we were treated here in Oasis, SCD finished building their community center. The place could have been heaven on earth, but it is a living hell instead. The president of the Sanctuary Council was seized for treason. And some say it was because of a libel suit fabricated by Richard Truman, who wanted to become president. Jim and his gang threatened not only me but also everybody else. People are so afraid of each other that nobody even uses the community center.

"See, on the evening I called you, I was frightened and desperate. After Jim said that he would kill me if I didn't make love to him the following day, I knew I had to leave at once, but I had nowhere to go. I hope that if you want me to go, you will give me some time to find another place to live."

"I don't blame you for not wanting to stay there, Charlotte. Whatever happens, I will never put you in harm's way."

CHAPTER 2

CALLAHAN

Oasis was one of the nine communities built by Sustainable Community Developers (SCD) across the United States. The idea was the brainchild of James Callahan, the owner and CEO of the company, who believed that people concerned about climate change would pay as much as they were able for a sustainable home, as long as the company could offer feasible options with regard to location and price.

The company's experts combed the country for potential sites for development. Callahan set the ideal criteria. The developments should be far from any large body of water, but close to a source of potable water, and far away from a large metropolitan area, but no more than an hour's drive from a medium-size city where residents would be able to find employment and access to services. The size of the development should be sufficient for about twenty families and include additional lots for nonresidential use.

Callahan, both engineer and businessman, hired the best sustainability experts he could find to ensure that all the communities had state-of-the-art renewable energy sources, mostly geothermal and solar energy based, although they were all connected to the local grid as well. All locations had an independent water system, which drew and filtered water from a nearby source, and a system to treat sewage water for irrigation. In areas blessed with a high level of precipitation, they designed sophisticated systems for collecting rain and snowmelt.

James Callahan also took pride in thinking about the social aspects of the small communities and insisted on building them around a multipurpose community center for meetings, education, sports, communal gatherings, meals, and whatever other needs that may arise. The foundations for these centers were built with the first units as a marketing ploy to justify the high price, but several centers were still under construction when the residents moved in.

SCD communications experts made sure to wire the homes to a state-of-the-art telecommunications system that connected all the residents both to a village network and to the outside world and provided means of communication and teleconferencing that were crucial when adverse weather or other environmental hazards prevented people from leaving their homes. Teaming with Residential Greenhouse, SCD offered several designs of greenhouses, accessible from home for residents who were willing and able to pay the extra price. Most were.

Although all locations were similar in functionality, they differed significantly in their level of luxury, ranging from basic three-bedroom units to luxurious five large bedrooms with all the amenities one could desire. The price range varied accordingly, but because of all the innovative features, all SCD homes were much more expensive than comparable homes in the nearby city. Therefore, they were not very popular. Only people who believed that this was the only key to survival purchased them.

Many buyers could not receive the needed loans from a bank or another lending company because their income was lower than the minimum requirement. They had to accept SCD's harsh payment schedule and find creative ways to pay the bills. They were moonlighting, living in unfurnished rooms, and trying to get free meals wherever they could. SCD was merciless; those who owed more than three monthly mortgage payments had to foreclose, which allowed SCD to resell the property. Callahan was not apologetic, believing he had the right to receive a proper return on his investment.

Callahan himself lived in Abundance, the upscale community he'd developed about one hundred miles west of the Atlantic coast. It allowed him to have his chauffeur drive him to Washington, DC, and if need be to use his private helicopter. He made sure that an exquisite community center was ready and equipped with all the amenities: pool, gym, kitchen appliances, and furniture for the big dining/meeting room and activity rooms. His neighbors were very wealthy people, much richer than he was, and they treated each other with haughty respect. Personally, he would have preferred less snobbism and a more genuine relationship between people, but he had to accept the situation as part of the deal. He was hoping that the forecasted hardships would draw people together and bring about the collaboration that is essential to survival.

Another thing SCD communities had in common was their bombastic names: Abundance, Prosperity, and Serenity in the East, or East, as the area was later referred to; Oasis, Sanctuary, and Refuge in the Central region, or Central; and Glamour, Charisma, and Gorgeous in the West, later referred to as West. People joked that the names reflected Callahan's opinion of each region, which was not far from the truth.

Two years ago, after the two-week-long natural disasters that left millions dead had hit, James Callahan decided to withdraw from his investments in central and western USA and concentrate on the three communities in the East. Although all the residents of the nine communities survived the disaster, he was not sure that he would be able to collect the money the residents still owed him should another calamity occur. Callahan presented the residents with a renewed contract that offered a significant rebate in return for paying the remainder of the mortgage in full. He figured that they would be able to borrow this amount from a local bank and be granted less arduous terms. To maximize his profit, he included a small-print clause that relieved him of his responsibility to complete the community center in the locations where one was still under construction.

He was right about the Central communities. These were the less luxurious ones, and the residents lived in constant fear of not being able to pay the mortgage. The foreclosure stories sufficed to convince the homeowners to make every sacrifice possible to have a roof over the heads of them and their loved ones. The renewed loans that spread over longer times and involved lower monthly payments were a breather for them, so they ignored this clause and arranged the local loans to meet the new contract.

However, Callahan was less lucky in the West. Only Gorgeous residents signed the new contract. Their community center was already built, and the affluent residents had no problem refinancing. For them, it was a win-win game. Charisma residents' lawyer succeeded in negotiating a better deal, one that forced Callahan to cut his losses and complete the community center before the contract was signed. The Glamour residents took their chances, hoping that the next disaster would cause transportation and communication problems that would prevent Callahan from collecting the payments or executing foreclosures.

Callahan's decision to stay in the East brought about unexpected changes in his life and company, as the Illuminati, or Order Defenders (OD), took power and as a result the elected president of the United States and his cabinet disappeared. Most people did not know who the OD were except that they were very wealthy people who could pay handsomely for surrogates to do the dirty work for them and maintain order. Exploiting the confusion and despair of the homeless who lost everything, the OD signed them up on work contracts obligating them to accept any work assigned to them and to work ten hours a day, six days a week, in exchange for food and shelter. Most of the weather-displaced refugees believed that they had no other choice. Only a few saw the trap and preferred life as a vagabond over slavery.

Callahan was asked by the OD to build the residential buildings for these people as fast as possible. They provided him with a horrific and unattractive design for the huge buildings, each containing many small apartments. They requested that he use his experience to ensure that the structures would withstand future disasters and be energy-efficient but that he not add any sustainability feature. The OD wanted the people to depend on them for the supply of food, water, and energy.

At first, Callahan took the bait and considered himself a hero helping the uprooted to find safe shelter. But as the new rulers' exploitation tactics became impossible to ignore, he realized that he had sold his soul to the devil. To be sure, he had never been the bleeding-heart type, but he could not believe he had allowed himself to reach this level of depravity. The price was right though. He was invited to become part of the elite, was promised to have as many work contracts as he could carry out, and enjoyed all the privileges of the Order Defenders. Once he became associated with the OD, any demonstration of hesitation or criticism meant a risk to his life and that of his family. His wife, Sophie, was miserable and detested what had become of him. His old friends mistrusted him and severed their relationship. But as much as he did not like it, he felt that there was no way out and that he had better comply.

Callahan was driving home after a long day of meeting with the Order Defenders' executive board, discussing future projects. They were very pleased with his work and even hinted that they were considering him as a potential new member of the group. It was very flattering, because Felix Atwell, the appointed puppet president of the United States, who attended the meeting as well, was not considered as a candidate. Still, something told Callahan that he should not be happy about this development. He felt a great urge to discuss it with Sophie, his wife of twenty years, but then he knew it was not safe to speak with her about these kinds of topics over the phone.

From a distance, he noticed that, unlike the neighbors' homes that were all lit as if there had not been an energy crisis, his home was as dark as a black hole, the only one in the neighborhood to be dark. He felt a chill in his body after he opened the garage door and saw that Sophie's car was not there. As soon as he entered his home, he turned all the lights on and looked frantically for a note explaining where his wife and son were. He found none.

The silence seemed hostile and terrifying. *Something is very wrong,* he thought. Then the sinister reality hit him. *It cannot be. Oh God, please don't let that have happened!* He entered the room of his seventeen-year-old son, Jacob, and noticed that the boy's beloved guitar, his communicator, and most of his clothes were gone. Checking the closet next to his bedroom revealed the same picture. His wife's best clothes and jewelry were gone as well.

His feelings fluctuated between anger and concern. *Sophie, why couldn't you have trusted me?* he lamented. Then he murmured, "I hope they are safe." Imagining his wife and son on their own in Central, he worried, *Did she take any money?* He ran to his communicator to check his finances and realized that about half a million dollars had disappeared from their joint account. To his surprise, he felt relieved. Being hungry, he was trying in vain to find something to eat in the empty refrigerator. *She could at least have left me a nice dinner!*

He knew that Sophie did not approve of his business relations with the Order Defenders, but he did not believe she would have run away without letting him know or, at the very least, leaving a note.

Contemplating where Sophie and Jacob might be right now, Callahan reasoned that if they left shortly after he went to work and hadn't been caught, they should now be in Central, away from the reaching hand of the Order Defenders, although nobody who left the Order Defenders could be safe anywhere.

A ringing phone startled him. It was Emily, Sophie's best friend. "Hi, Jimmy. May I talk with Sophie? There is something I need to tell her right away."

"Oh my God, Emily, I was sure she was with you! She said she was going to spend the day with you. I have just returned from my meeting to an empty home and meant to call you."

Emily's friendly voice turned cold and distant. "I have not seen her or Jacob for at least a week, and we did not have any plan to meet today either. Don't tell me she ran away from you."

James hung up, realizing that he could no longer keep Sophie's disappearance a secret and deciding that he should be tremendously cautious when communicating with others. The phone rang again. This time it was Jacob's teacher.

"Jacob did not show up in school today, and nobody has called the office to explain his absence. I am going to ignore the formalities. Just make sure that he shows up on time to school tomorrow, okay?"

Callahan knew that at this point telling the truth was his best defense. He'd attended meetings with the board all day and had an alibi.

"Sorry, Donna! I have just returned home from work. Neither Sophie nor Jacob is home. I am trying to figure out where they are."

"It does not sound good! I will have to report it to the principal tomorrow. Good luck!" she said. Then she hung up.

It was about 10:00 p.m. EST. Callahan figured that at 9:00 p.m.

CST, he could still make a phone call to Clara, Sophie's sister who lived in Oasis. He keyed the number.

"Hello, Jim," Clara said. "I will be very short. Sophie called earlier today. She and Jacob are somewhere in Central. She has no plans to come to Oasis or visit our sister Edna in Refuge. It would be too dangerous for her and us. She plans to disappear in Central and not contact any of us for a long time. She said she loves you but can no longer live with you or in any other place in the East."

"Thank you, Clara. My best wishes to you, Oasis, Refuge, and Sanctuary. If by any chance you hear from Sophie, tell her I love her too, and tell her that the way she left is unfair to me."

"You were unfair to her as well, and you know that. Anyway, it was her decision. Please don't try to look for her," warned Clara.

"I won't. It is too dangerous for me, her, and Jacob. Tell Jacob I will always love him. Good night."

He wondered how much Sophie knew about his sexual escapades when he was working in Colorado and California. Hearing from Clara that he had been unfair led him to the inevitable conclusion that she probably knew much more than he had hoped.

Even now, Callahan was not apologetic about his adventures. He fondly remembered himself as a young, bright, successful man to whom everything had come easily, wealth, women, and influence, and who believed that he deserved it all. Being tall, well-built, and handsome, he knew that many women were attracted to him, and not just because of his wealth. He remembered two of them who almost led him to divorce Sophie. Sometimes he thought that maybe he should have waited longer to get married, or at least at the age of thirty not to marry a nineteen-year-old.

However, the fifty-two-year-old who witnessed disasters and unfathomable suffering was no longer as self-righteous as he was twenty-odd years ago. He was happy to be alive, knowing well that everything he thought he could rely on is ephemeral and may vanish without warning. Although still attractive, he had not been with another woman for a long time, and he enjoyed the only place where he felt secure and loved—his home, with his wife and only child. Realizing that it was all gone and that his chance of finding them somewhere in Central was zilch, he felt a sharp pain in his chest and tried to halt a choking cry.

He knew it would not be long before he heard from the "Devil," but he was hoping it would not be until tomorrow. He got ready for bed, knowing that his life would no longer be the same.

The phone rang again. An angry voice sounded from the receiver.

"Callahan, Felix Atwell here. I have just heard about your wife and son. You really fooled all of us. You are no longer trusted. We are going to do no more business with you or SCD. I don't care what you do, but I suggest that you don't try to follow your wife and son. We will find you anywhere you go. Is that clear?"

"I won't follow them."

Atwell hung up before hearing the answer.

What am I going to do now? Callahan realized that there was a way out, Sophie had just taken it, but he preferred the route of compliance. Now he had no job or family, and the prospect of escape was suddenly much more dangerous. Being pragmatic, James decided that although it would be too dangerous to escape East now, he had better live as far from Washington, DC, as possible. Knowing the market for new homes and sustainability projects, he figured that his best bet would be to go south. One thing he would not regret was leaving his residence in Abundance. Although he had developed this luxurious community, the haughty residents who'd acquired the properties had always treated him as their servant, not their equal, and seemed to have tolerated him only because of his work with the OD.

The housing market was good, and Callahan knew that many people were interested in buying property in Abundance; hence, he could get an excellent price for his home. He contacted some potential buyers, hoping to finalize a deal quite quickly. Now that he was no longer an OD favorite, his neighbors were sure to treat him as a pariah, and he was surely not going to miss them.

Luckily, he had built two other communities in the East: Prosperity in the north and Serenity in the south. Although Clara's daughters, Sue and Amalia, lived in Prosperity with their families, thanks a great deal to his generous financial help, and even though he'd heard from them that Prosperity was a success story, under the current circumstances it was not the best time for a family reunion.

He did not like the idea of going north anyway, because the OD control of the Northeast was too tight, and his chance of escaping to

Central should he decide to do so was close to zero. It had been awhile since he'd visited Serenity, the community he'd built in Georgia. He hoped that it was thriving. *I need some serenity,* he thought, hoping that the community would live up to its name.

He contacted Serenity and found out that there was one property on the market. Its design was not one of the best, but he felt that anything in Serenity would do, given that he could not trust any other builder to build a structure that satisfied his criteria for safety and sustainability. And if he were to find a way to disappear, the less he invested in a home, the better. After all, any unit would suffice for one person, and he had no plans to start a new family anytime soon.

At least business turned out the way he expected. He sold his Abundance home within a month for an excellent price and got a fantastic deal on the property in Serenity. Two months after Sophie had left, he was on his way south.

CHAPTER 3

COMMUNITY IS BORN

The morning following Governor Hickman's presentation found Steve glued to his information screen, anxiously waiting for Rudolph's face to appear and open the teleconference meeting. Finally, five minutes after nine o'clock, he heard the familiar sound. A grim-faced Rudolph appeared on the screen.

"Good morning! I think Governor Hickman said it all. The question is, how do we organize to create a community in which we would all be proud to live? But before we start planning, I would like to know if anybody has any idea why Faithfield, of all places, was attacked by the Order Defenders. Clara, your brother-in-law works for them. Have you heard from him?"

"I did hear from Callahan. He no longer works for them, because his wife and son ran away to Central. To make a long story short, he now lives in Serenity and works on remodeling homes in Georgia and Florida, so he knows nothing about the OD plans. When he contacted me, I told him that Sophie, my sister, called me once to relate that she was safe somewhere in Central and was going to disappear so that they could not track her. I am sure that the OD wiretapped his phone and listened to this conversation. I must admit that the idea that the bombs were intended to reach us as some kind of punishment for our connection with James did cross my mind, but I cannot change the fact that Sophie is my sister."

"Thanks, Clara. I hope you will not hear from him again."

"Now, back to our agenda! In our last meeting, some people

suggested that although our skilled engineers and the owners of Sustainit, Mark and Donna, have taken care of all the machinery that provided us with energy, water, and connection to the world, we have never had a formally elected council. Quite frankly, I thought that for a twelve-family community, an informal organization would suffice, but in light of recent events, I agree that it may not be enough. I believe that I represent all of us when I thank Mark and Donna and ask if one of them will submit his or her candidacy to become our first elected president."

Donna's petite figure appeared on the screen. "Thank you all. We are honored by your proposition, but we must decline. With two kids and Sustainit to manage, we need no more responsibilities. Of course, we will continue taking care of Oasis resources. I am willing to submit my candidacy for a council member, but not for the president role. Since I have your attention, I want to mention that we are thinking about extending Sustainit beyond the development and production of devices for solar energy and protective screens. We are considering branching out to greenhouse building and installing as well, if we can secure more employees from Faithville. Given the dire climate situation, we would welcome any of our neighbors who are interested in working with us."

Rudolph thanked Donna and then reminded the listeners of the questionnaire he had sent them asking about their occupations and hobbies. He noted jokingly that some people like Fred the shop owner, Ralph the banker, Henry the builder, Dr. Grisham, and of course Rudolph himself needed no introduction. He said that all have enjoyed watching Oasis's talented actress Daphne in the movies and on advertisements. Then, after pausing for a minute, he added that all have enjoyed the dairy products produced by Bill and Liz, the community farmers.

"Beside them, we have three engineers, two social workers, and three wonderful active teachers, besides Stanley and Clara, who are retired teachers. We have one accountant, and many talented people such as a professional violinist, a yoga and Pilates instructor, and a painter or two. Quite impressive! If I forgot something, or if you would like to ask each other questions before the elections, now is the time to speak."

Steve did not feel any need to introduce himself, because he knew that people who had health issues would know to knock on his door. As a matter of fact, the only people whom he knew more than superficially were the ones who did have medical issues. He reminisced about the night Clara had knocked on his door and begged him to see her husband, Stanly, who had breathing problems. He recalled how impressed he'd been by the way these two retirees looked at each other, and by their warm and considerate relationship. He was concerned about Stanly's health but fascinated with the man's wisdom and knowledge, which made Steve think that he might be a good president. *I wish I had that kind of relationship,* he'd thought, glancing at Charlotte, who sat on a chair away from the sofa and hardly said anything. Oh, and the fresh cake Clara had him take home when he refused to accept money from a friend! He could still taste it in his mouth.

Then he remembered how he'd had to improvise when Tim, the older son of Bill and Liz, broke his leg when the boys were playing football on the unbuilt lots of the community. Liz insisted on giving him the grand tour of the farm, the barn, and the small cheese factory, and then she'd made him take home eggs, milk, and cheese sufficient for two weeks.

And how could he forget all the kids who had caught the flu whom he was called to help!

Henri's appearance caused Steve to return his gaze to the screen. Henri probably spoke for a long time, but Steve only heard him saying, "I have already arranged for some workers to come and start building the community center this weekend. I would like all of you to attend and assist in the building. Also, before Saturday, please pay the two thousand dollars due to whomever we elect as treasurer during this conference."

That made Steve check his calendar, verifying that his shift did not fall on Saturday, and lament about all the things he had planned to do for his garden and research that would have to wait. Then he heard Laura, an elementary schoolteacher and Henri's wife, arguing that it was not safe to send the young children to Faithville schools, and that once the community center was built, it should also serve as a mini preschool and elementary school. Steve did not have children, but knowing at least some of them in his community, he thought that Laura's proposal was a good idea.

When Fred boasted of his accomplishments, Steve could not avoid grinning widely. Every time he ordered unusual items for his lab or garden, which he often did, he would receive a big lecture about how Fred's ingenuity allowed him to find the rare items and get them for Steve swiftly and at a good price. Steve had to admit that this exaggerated self-congratulation was not unsubstantiated.

Surprise! Charlotte pressed the button and declared that her hobby was painting and that she could decorate the community center after its completion. Steven wondered about this, having never seen her paint or even have canvas, paints, or brushes in her possession.

Then, he noticed Daphne's fragile figure, gentle expression, and beautiful long blonde hair as she informed the community that, being concerned about having found herself out of work as an actress, she had started studying horticulture and TV programming at Faithfield University. Her dream, she added, was to produce a weekly educational program that informs people how to live sustainably. *I wonder if she would show up in my class or invite me as a guest on her program,* he thought, smiling to himself.

Rudolph's face appeared on the screen.

"It's great that we enjoy communicating with each other, and maybe we should do it more often, but now it's election time. First, let's elect a president. I nominate Stanly Steiner."

"Second," yelled Ralph.

"Are there additional nominations? Everybody can select any adult, including him- or herself." Rudolph waited for a few minutes, and when he could no longer bear the silence, he said, "Each of the twenty-two adults will vote by saying 'aye,' 'nay,' or 'abstain.'"

The total was twenty ayes and two abstentions, so Stanly became the first president of Oasis Council. Vanessa, the accountant, was selected as treasurer; Laura, a teacher, as education coordinator; Fred, the store owner, as food and supply coordinator; Rudolph as communications coordinator; Donna as building and energy coordinator; and Daphne as cultural coordinator.

Rudolph appeared again on the screen. "We accomplished a lot today. I hope that you will all support our council and help when asked to do so. I foresee some ad hoc committees for ad hoc issues such as health. But for the sake of not including all of us on the council, we will see how it works. We may make some changes for the next election.

"This concludes our meeting today. See you all on Saturday morning, ready to work at the community center, with some goodies for a potluck. As of now, the weather forecast is good, so we can have picnic tables outside. God bless Oasis!"

Thank God nobody nominated me for anything, thought Steve, who was relieved but quite insulted that nobody had recognized his contribution to the health of the community. *They sure know how to find me when they need help.* He was somewhat grumpy, but other than that, he was satisfied with the outcome of the election.

Oasis Map

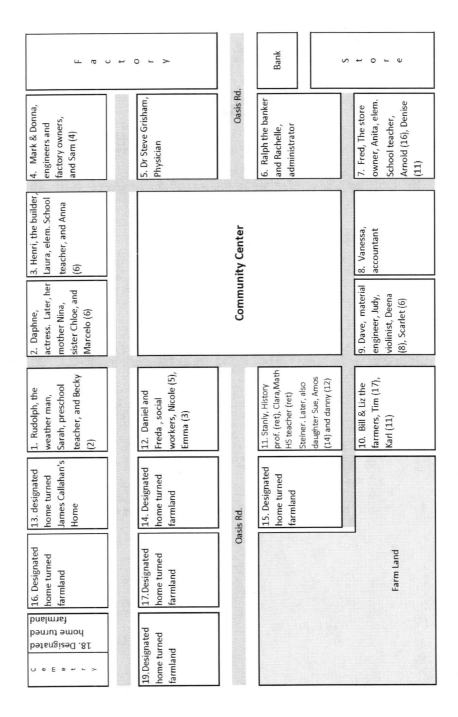

Factory

2. Daphne, actress. Later, her mother Nina, sister Chloe, and Marcelo (6)

3. Henri, the builder, Laura, elem. School teacher, and Anna (6)

4. Mark & Donna, engineers and factory owners, and Sam (4)

1. Rudolph, the weather man, Sarah, preschool teacher, and Becky (2)

13. designated home turned James Callahan's Home

16. Designated home turned farmland

18. Designated home turned farmland cemetery

Oasis Rd.

5. Dr Steve Grisham, Physician

Community Center

12. Daniel and Freda, social workers, Nicole (5), Emma (3)

14. Designated home turned farmland

17. Designated home turned farmland

19. Designated home turned farmland

Oasis Rd.

Bank

Store

6. Ralph the banker and Rachelle, administrator

7. Fred, The store owner, Anita, elem. School teacher, Denise Arnold (16), Denise (11)

8. Vanessa, accountant

9. Dave, material engineer, Judy, violinist, Deena (8), Scarlet (6)

11. Stanly, History prof. (ret), Clara, Math HS teacher (ret) Steiner. Later, also daughter Sue, Amos (14) and danny (12)

10. Bill & Liz the farmers, Tim (17), Karl (11)

15. Designated home turned farmland

Farm Land

Saturday morning turned out to be a bright, beautiful day suitable for the construction project. Steve was looking forward to it impatiently. He sensed that something wonderful was manifesting before his eyes, and for the first time he felt proud of his community. He also felt that the sacrifices that he, as well as his neighbors, had made to buy the property had not been in vain. He recalled that before the last conference calls, especially after his visit to Sanctuary, he'd had concerns about the community's cohesiveness that he had never expressed in public. Now he sadly acknowledged that this wonderful transformation he was seeing become manifest, would have happened with or without him.

What kind of cocoon am I living in? he thought. What bothered him most was the fact that he'd said nothing about the need to equip the community center with greenhouses and raise crops that individual residents could not raise in their smaller greenhouses, not to mention the need to increase the amount of food that the community as a whole produced. He had many plans running through his head to do so, but he'd kept them all to himself. Now, he was determined to change this fact. Seeing Charlotte in the kitchen baking her favorite bread and preparing a huge bowl of salad, he bitterly thought that at least she was doing something to contribute to the event.

Once everything was prepared, Steve and Charlotte crossed the path separating their home and the community center. Steve noticed that most of the residents had already arrived. He approached Mark and Donna, who were busy giving instructions to some of their employees and some volunteers for the installation of the solar panels, the rainwater collection tank, and protective shield-all products manufactured by their Sustainit factory. Visibly distressed, he was waiting for a right moment to speak with one of them privately. Mark led the group to the roof, and Donna turned to Steve.

"Good morning, Doc. Where have you been?"

"I was waiting to have a moment to speak with you about something very important ..."

"I saw you, Steve. I meant, where were you during our last meeting? I was waiting to hear a big lecture about nutrition, similar to what I'd heard from you when my son Sam was sick and you prescribed those strange herbs. And I was stunned that you were silent during the entire discussion and said nothing about the need to add greenhouses to the community center. Don't you care about our community?"

"That is what I wanted to talk to you about," said Steve sheepishly.

"Well, it's good that at least one of us thought about it ahead of time. I am Oasis's building and energy coordinator, and I take this responsibility seriously. I spoke with Henri and, after clarifying with Vanessa that we have the money, decided to order two large greenhouses from Colorado Greenhouses, the company we work with. They are going to be here soon. The people at Colorado Greenhouses are experienced and have some plans about what to plant in the greenhouses, but I prefer that at least one of us have a say. And I appoint you. You can use part of the greenhouses for your experiments. Just promise me that you are not going to fill them with mushrooms and herbs."

Steve was not too happy with the way she was treating him, although he knew that he should have voiced his opinions earlier.

"I know what we need to grow, and I will do it, but I suggest to add Liz, who has experience raising the type of crops that I do not have in my greenhouse."

"Good idea. Why don't you talk to her?" she replied. Then she disappeared to help her husband with the installations.

Steve had not mentioned adding Bill, Liz's husband, to the team because he sensed that he would be able to work well with her but probably not with him. He had not seen her this morning, so he peeped into the community center, where Henri, his worker, and some volunteers were busy setting the tiles for the floor and painting the first level. Judging from the noise coming from the basement, he guessed that some work was being done down there as well. He asked around, but none of the people in the building had seen Liz.

So he left the building, watching the young children playing joyously under the tutelage of the community teachers, whom he saw in his mind as the future teachers of the community school. He headed toward the picnic tables, where Charlotte, Clara, and Vanessa had started organizing the potluck food. He asked about Liz and was told by Clara that she was busy on her farm and would arrive later.

Determined to find her, and ignoring Charlotte's disapproving looks, Steve started walking toward her residence. Once he arrived, he caught her coming out her door. He'd hardly had a chance to explain their new assignment when they heard the heavy noise of the truck moving slowly along Oasis's narrow trails.

"Let's go, Liz. Here they are."

To his surprise, she did not hurry to join him. Instead, she turned to the three older boys of the community, two of which were hers, who were standing not far away, and asked them to help. They willfully joined Steve and Liz, still talking about school and discussing how to convince the council to build a soccer field on the property. Steve wondered whether they would help more than stand in the way.

He greeted the Colorado Greenhouses team manager and worker and presented Liz and himself as Oasis representatives. Liz hurried to introduce the three boys as well. The manager suggested that his workers and the boys set the prebuilt structures while his expert discussed with Liz and Steve the details about the crops to be planted.

Liz and Steve first listened to the company's expert plan and agreed to a great deal of it. Steve was pleased to hear that they had brought a variety of fruit trees from their nursery. Liz suggested planting some grains like quinoa. Steve nodded, as that was exactly what he'd intended to suggest. The manager apologized for the fact that they were short of seeds.

Steve felt that he must seize the moment. He told the group that he had a seed collection of quinoa and other grains and also of a variety of very nutritious vegetables that were not sold in the stores. He also asked for a small area for his experiments, explaining how the things he grew helped him cure many diseases. To his surprise, the manager showed a lot of interest in his research and noted that he would discuss the matter with his supervisor and recommend that Steve collaborate with their researchers. Liz said she would love to plant some of his seeds on her farm. Steve started feeling better and walked to his lab to fetch the seeds. Finally, he felt a part of the community.

At noon all broke for a great lunch. The Oasis women had definitely tried to show off their skills, given the tasty casseroles, fresh loaves of bread, homemade fruit preserves, and colorful salads that garnished the table.

They all continued working diligently after the short lunch, and at the end of the day, the building was unrecognizable. The roofing with the solar panel was complete. The rooms were all painted, the floor was set, and light fixtures cast a pleasant light. The basement was finished, with a beautiful pool waiting to be tested, along with men's and women's locker rooms with showers and toilets. All it needed was some benches and workout machines. On the first floor, the kitchen was operable, and one large assembly hall and seven smaller activity rooms were all ready to be furnished and used.

Steve looked lovingly at the two large greenhouses, complete with irrigation and weather-control systems, knowing that the right crops for the community were planted in the appropriate soil. He felt that his knowledge and expertise, as well as his seeds, had contributed to the community's future. And Donna was not the only person to pat him on the shoulder.

Daphne and Charlotte brought some of their pictures to decorate the assembly hall and the spaces for the future school. Steve asked himself where Charlotte had hidden these pictures until now.

Then they all stood around Stanly Steiner, the community elder and new president, and his wife, Clara. Steve, who had not indulged in any of life's small pleasures like a good wine for a long time, smiled when Stanly opened a bottle of champagne that he had kept for the occasion. Clara poured it into small cups. Steve drank and cheered with everyone gathered. Stanly announced a meeting next Saturday at ten and promised that by then, he and Vanessa would have purchased tables, chairs, and what was needed for the kitchen.

Steve and Charlotte walked back home wordlessly, immersed in their thoughts. Steve wondered about the apparent relationship between Charlotte and Vanessa. He knew that Vanessa had a guest room that she could rent. Considering the possibility of Charlotte's moving there, he was surprised that he did not find the idea upsetting. Quite the opposite; he was relieved. Steve realized that the relationship between him and Charlotte could never have worked. It had been based solely on mutual convenience. He was certainly not her dream man, and she, although very attractive and efficient, was far from being his soul mate.

As they entered home and turned on the lights, Charlotte said, "Steve, we need to talk." "Yes," he answered, "we sure do." Steve's hunch had been correct. Charlotte had talked with Vanessa about renting her guest room. She thought that her position would allow her to afford the rent, and leaving Steve would set her free to look for somebody she could love. She told Steve that Vanessa could use the money, recognizing that her position was insecure and that each calamity made it more likely that the financial consulting company she worked for would go under. She also mentioned that in spite of the fact that Vanessa was twenty years older than she, the two got along very well.

Charlotte expected Steve to be surprised and upset to hear the news. She was sure he would beg her to stay. When he just said "okay," she was taken aback. She could not understand why he'd traveled to Sanctuary to bring her back if he did not care. The truth was that Steve could not fathom it either.

Just before he fell asleep, it occurred to Steve that he had noticed Rudolph and Clara discussing something at length. He wondered what it might be.

--------◆◆◆◆◆◆--------

The following morning, Clara knocked on the door to Rudolph's lab. He let her in and, without resorting to small talk, invited her to sit in front of his grand wooden desk, where she could hardly see him over the big computer and a variety of instruments the function of which she could not fathom. Clara was known to Oasis residents as the wise old woman, or crone, who conducted shamanic drumming sessions in her home on the first Saturday of each month, and performed divination sessions using a pendulum, tarot cards, and other methods. Her shamanic journey sessions were attended mostly by women, and occasionally by a few men who seemed to have been dragged there by their wives. Rudolph had never attended any of the sessions, but his wife, Sara, had, and she had always returned home after a session happy and inspired. So he'd decided to seek Clara's advice as a long shot, arranging their meeting the day before.

Clara was looking curiously at the strange instruments. She asked how they worked, but Rudolph impatiently cut her short and asked if she'd had any success in identifying the spy who broadcasted messages containing confidential information from Oasis back to East.

She replied that she had journeyed and seen cows and heard their mooing. A strong wind was carrying the sound eastward. She was sure the spy was Bill, the farmer, and she believed that his wife, Liz, was unaware of his activities.

Rudolph looked disappointed. He'd received information from the state intelligence agency about their suspicion that a spy in Oasis was broadcasting information to East. On a hunch, he had decided to use Clara's psychic abilities first, before using his instruments to follow the activities of each residential unit. He had wanted to start with the best bet, but now he was not convinced that he'd made the right choice.

"Clara, no wonder you heard cows. The farmer is your neighbor. And what exactly do you mean by journeyed?"

Clara was apparently upset. "Rudolph, I am not stupid or a lunatic! Believe it or not, I had the same idea. So, after my vision ended, I went outside. I could not hear the cows. I saw them grazing at the farthest corner of Bill's lot, and the wind was carrying whatever sound the cows might have made in the opposite direction. Also, for additional validation, I used divination with a pendulum. Same results. All the other residents came up as a no; only Bill was a yes. Now, since Sarah apparently has not told you, journeying is kind of meditation using drums, which help the practitioner to enter an alternate reality and access the help of all sorts of guides, helpers, and teachers. I really don't want to go into more details, as you don't seem to appreciate it anyway."

"I deeply apologize. I will use your vision and see what I can do with it."

Clara got up and left without saying goodbye.

CHAPTER 4

TURNING POINT

James Callahan returned to his Serenity home after a business trip to Florida. He did not bother to stop and have a small chat with his neighbors, who looked at him suspiciously, or even wave to them. He entered the garage and closed the door behind him. He had a hard time believing that living in a place called Serenity was a problem. What he faced there turned the name he had lovingly given the development into an ironic misnomer. Rather than becoming a cohesive community, Serenity became the hub of two competing cliques, each led by one of the richest families. Each group had its own meetings, parties, and other organized activities. When members of the competing groups happened to meet in the community gym, they avoided each other to the best of their ability. Children of both groups were not allowed to play together either. Callahan had not expected that the community would be divided along Anglo and Hispanic ethnic lines, but such was the reality he encountered. Neither of these groups accepted him, as they both believed he was an Order Defenders' spy, not to mention that he did not like either of the groups.

The problems with Serenity led him to enjoy leaving home and going south for extended periods of time to carry out his sustainable energy projects. Local funds provided resources for rebuilding some of the homes destroyed by the hurricanes that had hit the state a few months prior, and Callahan was proud to be part of the reconstruction. In the evenings he would visit bars, cafes, restaurants, and clubs to listen to conversations and get a feel for the people's mood. Meeting new people under the veil of anonymity was a delight. Moreover, this was his opportunity to listen to rumors and personal stories, which was crucial given the misleading information provided by the government-controlled media. And the rumors had become exponentially worse.

He was concerned about the rise of hate groups and the growing number of heavily armed survivalist communities around. He knew that in spite of the fact that all of them hated the OD, they were not the right groups to liberate the country from the secret organization. Callahan could not decide whom he was more afraid of, the survivalists or the OD. Both of these groups cared about themselves and hated everybody else. The resistance should evolve from among ingenious and honest people, but could it? Would it? Since there was so much to be afraid of, everybody lived in fear.

Realizing that it took his having been forced to leave his work with the OD to hear this information, Callahan could not comprehend how he could have ignored what was going on around him for so long, caring only about his work and family. *Now I have neither,* he thought bitterly. Being a proud businessman and the most in-demand community developer, he had enjoyed his success, fame, good connections, and all the included fringe benefits tremendously. He had been unapologetic about it as unapologetic can be. Now, however, he started questioning his modus vivendi. He might have saved his marriage and escaped East, or at least stayed away from the OD's reach, had he kept his eyes open and stopped ignoring the atrocities committed by the OD before he'd become deeply involved with them. Pictures of parents overworking obediently to provide required health services for a sick child or make sure there was food on the table crossed his mind. *The OD control all the resources, and people have no choice other than to accept their own misery. How on earth could I have been part of it?*

During this last visit, the business was good, but the news was horrendous. Wherever Callahan went, whether to a cafe, bar, restaurant, or venue for a business meeting, people whispered the same horror stories as if fearful to hear what they were saying. He heard that the OD were becoming more vicious every day. People who dared to question their legitimacy or activities, and people who were caught trying to escape to Central, were tortured and killed, and their families were punished as well. People were describing the barbarism of the OD private mercenary army. Some cooperating generals had helped the OD take control of US Armed Forces bases from Maine in the north, to North Carolina in the south, to the Mississippi River to the west. So far, they had not been able to overthrow the local governments of the Southeast. It was clear that this would be their next step. Folks wondered if their governors and legislatures would have the willingness and power to resist. Many people had lost hope and decided to escape to the other side of the Mississippi before it was too late.

Callahan's scariest encounter happened in the last bar he'd gone to. A drunk lab worker or researcher had told the barman about experiments in genetics, something previously unthinkable to do.

"Until now I was working on curing diseases and preventing birth defects, and we were all very cautious not to mess up with engineering human traits. I know that some labs did illegally help athletes, or parents who wanted a beauty queen or a genius, but we have never done that. Now the OD has forced us to develop a method to create 'the perfect child' on the one hand and a docile, obedient child on the other. We perform some of the work in the lab with a natural birth. We do some experiments on orphans, victims of the latest disasters. It's terrible! The obedient children do not look like children at all. They hardly smile and they don't play; they just wait to be told what to do. We killed their curiosity. And you know what? The OD think that they can use these techniques on anyone considered to be a troublemaker. They can do it to me, to you, and to you too," he said, pointing to Callahan.

Callahan was shaken but managed to ask about the fate of the "perfect" children.

"They are not well either. They seem confused. Some show signs of schizophrenia. Some misbehave. Making too many changes without understanding how it all works together turns the result unpredictable and, most likely, far from what is desired. And these poor kids are treated like rats. They need a family. I had never thought I would be ashamed of what I am doing." He sobbed loudly and gulped down another drink.

The impassive face of the barman urged Callahan to pay the

bill and find his way out swiftly. As Callahan walked to his car, he had a strong feeling that somebody was following him. He looked around. There was nobody in the parking lot besides him. Looking backward again, he saw his long shadow. *Have I reached the point of being afraid of my own shadow?*

Although the business was excellent, and although he loathed the thought of moving again, Callahan knew he had to act fast before the OD decided to come after him.

✦✦✦✦✦✦

Felix Atwell set in the Oval Office, his new headquarters at the White House. He felt that finally he was where he was destined to be, the leader of the USA, although at that point it included just the eastern part. Moreover, he only had a partial understanding of the situation in the southeast, because his staff was afraid to tell him it was not under his full control. His people were hoping that the private army would take command of the situation soon.

He was aware, however, that many of the OD farms and factories were in need of more workers and that he was responsible for forcefully relocating people to the desired destinations. Because of the disasters, many of the robotic systems had malfunctioned and consequently were dismantled or had to undergo comprehensive restructuring and repair. So the OD needed people to do the robots' jobs and also to build new robotic systems. Atwell knew that there was only one person who could get it done. He hated his guts, but he was sure he could control him.

"Get me James Callahan at once," he yelled to his aide. Norma entered the room taking small hesitant steps. She could hear the signs of impatience and anger in his voice, usually harbingers of a temper tantrum.

She clicked Callahan's number. The silence was menacing. She tried again—same result. She called the communication manager and asked what was wrong. Atwell could overhear the answer. They could not reach Callahan's telephone any way they tried, probably because somebody had destroyed it.

"Get somebody from surveillance here, and do it fast!" Atwell yelled to Norma.

A minute later, Alfredo entered the president's office, visibly terrified, and set his computer on a small desk in the corner of the room. He started typing nervously on his keyboard, and informed Atwell that Callahan's car was in Florida and had been at the same location for three days.

"What location is it?" Atwell barked, moving toward the desk of a now petrified Alfredo. He looked at the screen. There was no mistake. Just above Callahan's car, there was a big sign that read: Krueger's Used Car Sale. "Did you get any signal at his home?" Atwell asked, not waiting for an answer. He knew very well that Callahan was already somewhere in Central. He wondered if Callahan had coordinated this scenario with his wife, Sophie, before she ran away.

Suddenly it occurred to him that the fact that Callahan had succeeded at overcoming the surveillance indicated, first, that Atwell's surveillance services were inadequate, to say the least, and second, that the OD hold on Florida, and maybe other states east of the Mississippi, was not as stable as he had been led to believe.

"Call Claudio Serafino, please," he said to Norma, realizing he had better win people's hearts instead of just spreading fear.

After Norma made some phone calls, she finally declared, "The general is on his way!"

Claudio Serafino had been the chairman of the Joint Chiefs of Staff under the legally elected President Rockwell. After the mysterious disappearance of the president, the secession of the central states, and the inability to effectively gain any control over the West, Serafino stayed in his post, coordinating what was left of the US Armed Forces with the OD's private army. Some of the generals had moved west and were quickly replaced; some had stayed. Serafino was not happy about the new order, but he realized that at this point it was too late to change horses.

"I want a full report of our surveillance capacity. How is it that James Callahan, who was under priority one surveillance, succeeded so easily in fooling us? How is it that he disappeared without anybody noticing at surveillance centers or the border?"

Serafino explained that their budget allowed for bugging people's homes, offices, cars, and phones but said that if a person gets rid of those bugs, it is hard to locate him or her. In the case of priority one surveillance, they also used drone reconnaissance, but there were not enough staff to analyze the results. He told Atwell that he'd found Callahan's whereabouts as revealed by the drone. Callahan crossed the Mississippi River yesterday and seemed to be on his way to Texas. At that point, they no longer know where he was. Serafino added that the army had many disciplinary issues and had had a hard time establishing control in the South. They could not assign more resources to surveillance.

"I will submit my resignation tomorrow," he said.

"Don't even think about it!" said Atwell, knowing very well that none of the few generals still in service would do a better job than Serafino. "I appreciate your honest report and your actions to rectify the shortcomings you mentioned. I will not accept a resignation!"

"Thanks for your trust," replied Serafino in a meek voice. Then he left the room.

"Norma, please get me General Albert Kraus," he asked Norma on the phone.

After a few minutes, she called Atwell, letting him know that General Kraus was in Massachusetts but that she had him on the phone.

Atwell knew that he did not have many marbles left to play with and had better be on good terms with the general, maybe offer him a raise. Still, he had to sound reassuring and self-confident if he wanted to maintain Kraus's respect and obedience.

"Hello, General. I know you are very busy up there, but I have a problem and would like to hear your suggestions. One of the people under our surveillance, whom I need for building projects in Florida and Georgia, escaped to Central, and if I had not asked for him, nobody would have noticed. Any idea how we can improve our dismal surveillance? A good idea and carrying it out would be handsomely rewarded."

"I heard about Callahan, Mr. President, and I am not surprised. We are busy chasing thousands of people who have attempted an escape to Central, as you ordered us, and have no workforce to establish the OD control in the South. So, my first suggestion is to let anybody who wants to leave to do so and keep track only of those categorized as priority one. Second, we have to be less hard on the people so that they will stop running away and start cooperating with the system. More resources would help upgrade our electronic surveillance, which is long overdue, but this in and of itself will not suffice."

It was the first time Atwell had heard criticism of his decisions coming from Kraus. He knew that Kraus would not have dared to speak to him with such disrespect unless he had the backing of Arnold Oliphant, chairman of the OD Council, who lived with his family in the OD Hub. Probably the news about Callahan had already reached Oliphant and he'd related it to Kraus. That meant that at least one of the people who knew about Callahan's disappearance—either Norma, his aide; Alfredo from surveillance; or General Serafino—had strong connections with Oliphant and kept him posted about important news and events. It was not forbidden, of course, but it implied that at least some of Atwell's people were not loyal to him.

"Of course I can improve people's living conditions, but it will cost the OD a lot of money. Is that what Oliphant wants?"

"I cannot speak on his behalf, Mr. President. I am waiting for your orders."

Atwell thanked him. He wondered if it would be better to contact Oliphant at once, which might make him look too anxious and insecure, or to wait a few hours.

A phone's ringing broke the silence. It was Norma, telling him that Oliphant was on the other line. With a deep sigh, he instructed her to put him on.

"We are going to have an emergency meeting at five o'clock in the Hub. Please be there on time," he said, with no greeting or introduction. Atwell glanced at his computer. The time was 12:05. He knew it was about a one-and-a-half-hour drive, so he had no time to waste; he had better be ready.

"Norma, please fetch Arthur and let him know that I need a ride this afternoon at three o'clock to the Hub." While waiting for confirmation, he sifted through financial, housing, and military reports and looked for any recent briefing on national and international affairs. He was not certain about the accuracy of these documents, but he had no better sources of information.

Norma knocked softly on the door and entered the room.

"Sorry to interrupt, Mr. President. It seems that Arthur disappeared as well. Nobody has seen him around for the last three days. When I called him, I received a message that the number is no longer in service. Should I find you another driver?"

"No, I will drive myself. Tell surveillance to assign priority one to find him and keep me posted. Oh, please keep my travel secret. If somebody asks about me, tell them I am in a meeting or something. If Oliphant calls, let him know that I am on my way."

Atwell knew that if Arthur, who was his driver and bodyguard and the only staffer who knew the way to the Hub, had defected to Central, then the Hub's location was no longer a secret. He could not risk involving another driver, so as much as he dreaded it, he knew he should drive himself.

Atwell entered his armored car wishing he could be with his wife and children instead of meeting Oliphant. Grief-stricken, he was driving to the secret location of the Hub, looking around to make sure that nobody was following him, ignoring the beauty of this fall day, the large trees adorned with leaves of yellow, orange, and red. He attempted to overcome his growing apprehension by telling himself that the OD Council had selected him unanimously as president of the United States to replace President Rockwell. He also recalled that Arnold Oliphant, the OD chief, had promised that the OD's private army's surveillance arm would protect him as much as it protected OD members as long as he stayed loyal.

But only now did he realize that, having been blinded by the great news, he had not bothered to inquire why they had decided to elect him as president and not one of their own. For a moment he was almost paralyzed, a horrifying idea having crossed his mind. They might have wanted to stay hidden, gaining power and enriching themselves, while he was the one who was exposed to the resulting hatred and criticism. He knew that they had the means to pay salaries and make sure that the generals were loyal to them, not to him. They were the ones who had authorized and carried out the military operations against Central. They had also dictated the plans for the residences designed and built by Callahan and others, and had received the revenues from the slave labor. But people would blame him, not the OD, for the bombing of Faithfield and the misery of the workers. And if he was not careful, his fate would be the same as Rockwell's.

He wondered what had happened to Rockwell, but all his

inquiries had been met by a "the less you know, the better" answer. Atwell was determined to be wiser and be ready to forsake the job. At that point, he knew he could not go west and that he had nowhere to hide, so he decided that he should continue to play his old unsuspicious self and see what happened.

He arrived at the Hub fifteen minutes before five o'clock, underwent the security check, and was directed to take the elevator down to the meeting room. Oliphant and most of the council members were already sitting around the dark wooden oval table, savoring the colorful fresh fruits, croissants, sandwiches, and pastries. Atwell remembered that he'd had nothing to eat since breakfast, and felt irresistible hunger. So, after greeting the councilmen, he helped himself to a full plate, thinking that he would need all the energy he could gather for the challenge.

As usual, Oliphant started with no pleasantries. "Atwell, I heard you drove yourself here. I hope nobody has identified you. That's not how I expect the president of the United States to behave. Explain, please!"

"My dear fellows." Atwell did his best to look serious but self-confident and presidential. "I am glad to see all of you, or rather most of you, as there are many things we need to discuss. To answer your question, Oliphant, yes, I drove myself, since my driver Arthur, the one who knows the way to the Hub, who has the highest level of security clearance, just disappeared and surveillance has no idea of his whereabouts. I happened to find this out shortly after discovering that James Callahan, our former builder, who was under the highest surveillance level, has already crossed the Mississippi on his way to Texas. I could not have taken the risk of involving another driver in a trip to our meeting. I wonder what we can do about our inadequate surveillance."

"Thank you, Atwell, for your good judgment," Oliphant responded. "The reason you do not see Manning here is that we were very displeased with his performance as director of intelligence and surveillance. We took care of him. I had planned to present him later, but since you asked, please meet our new director, Ernest Sullivan. Felix," he said, addressing Atwell uncharacteristically by using his first name, "feel free to discuss with him any concerns you have, and please report swiftly to me any problem before it turns into a disaster. You have my and the council's full support."

"Congratulations, Ernest. Let's get together soon to see what can be done to improve security," said Atwell as nonchalantly as he could, taking into consideration the chill he felt when Oliphant had talked about taking care of Manning. He wondered if the other absent council members were "being taken care of" as well. Oliphant made a move to continue, and the room became silent.

"As you all know, events did not turn out as we had planned. Our friends in Central and West were not as successful as we had expected in taking control of local and state governments. Our attack on Faithfield was very premature and unnecessarily exposed us. That was what helped Hickman create the coalition of the willing states who rescinded their allegiance to the union. He started with four states, and within two weeks sixteen other states west of the Mississippi, excepting California, joined. All we have now is the East, and even this is uncertain. We have already taken care of Elmore, who was in charge of law and order, making sure our Order spread around the country. The inner OD circle has just appointed our dear friend Louis Polk as his replacement. Atwell, please make sure you work with him as well."

Noticing that Polk looked more like a sacrificial lamb than a proud executor of OD control, Atwell promised to do so. He asked to know where California stood, not realizing that by so doing, he exposed his inability to receive the information required to perform his job.

"Friends," said Oliphant, "California is almost a Chinese colony."

Atwell, surprised by the blunt statement, looked around at the astonished looks on the other attendees' faces. It was clear to him that he was not the only one who had been kept in the dark. Apparently, Oliphant realized the same thing, because he announced his decision to begin a newsletter that would give everybody in the circle the appropriate information.

"As you know very well, we were not capable of assisting California when it was hit by multiple disasters. Chinese businesses had already bought a lot of companies and real estate in California and had made sure that the governor who was elected, Wang, was Chinese. Wang asked for help from the Chinese government.

They agreed, under the condition that California accept Chinese immigrants and grant them citizenship. So, China sent several contractors to rebuild residences for the survivors and to help establish the Chinese immigrants, carefully selected by the government, on Chinese-owned properties and on the land of people who had perished in the disasters. So, now they pretty much control the state."

Atwell was not the only one in the room who was thinking that the Chinese had done the same thing as the OD had, only better and with more generosity. Oliphant might have sensed this, because he redirected the discussion toward policy and guideline issues.

CHAPTER 5

FAITHFIELD STATE UNIVERSITY

Dr. Steve Grisham was on his way to teach his nutrition class. He loved what he called his escapades from the hospital to the university hallways and lecture rooms. Although he had dedicated his entire life to taking care of the sick, he realized that being among young healthy people felt like a breath of fresh air. And besides, he preferred instructing people to avoid diseases over curing them. He felt that the university's unique mission was compatible with his vision of what the mission of public higher education should be.

Faithfield State University (FSUni) had always taken pride in its service to the community. Faculty members were not expected to win prizes of excellence in their field or to publish in elite scientific journals. There was no money to pay for renowned academics in any case. But they were expected to provide support to their ten thousand or so students and the community.

With this mind-set, the university started reorganizing to meet the new reality. Administrators designed a maximally flexible curriculum. Students could take each class face-to-face, online, or with a combination of both modes. The curriculum enabled students to study at their own pace, and FSUni offered jobs related to their majors, as well as other necessary jobs to assist with the cost of living. Lab schedules were flexible, as were the dates of student evaluations, a.k.a. tests. So, students could take advantage of inclement weather conditions that prevented them from working outside their shelters so as to expedite their studies and write term papers, and then work extra hours when weather conditions improved. This flexibility put an enormous additional burden on faculty, but most were happy to be alive and to support the university endeavor.

The Engineering Department headed the project of repairing the campus buildings and student residences that had withstood the storms, also fortifying them to avoid future damage. Roofs and windows were protected, as were the water, energy, and food supply systems. The engineers added a new geothermal facility to the existing one to make sure the university was energy-independent and could even assist the city in an emergency. Faculty provided the design, and all assisted in carrying out the project.

The Department of Agriculture and Horticulture was busy building several greenhouse designs and experimenting with crops. They used the newest materials and technologies to ensure that the greenhouses could survive the storms. Greenhouses had been in high demand during the last five years, and there was a pressing need to provide the population with guidance about crop selection and maintenance and how to maximize the yield. In addition to the educational value of the new additions, the new greenhouses were expected to allow the university to produce the food used in its restaurants and cafeterias and to help feed the people who had fled the disasters.

The Academic Council, acknowledging that survival requires people to live more sustainably, and shifting students' choices of a major, upgraded the horticulture and nutrition programs and added climatology and survival classes.

Amid this state of affairs, Dr. Steve Grisham, the holistic physician, herbalist, and nutrition researcher, had become an overnight star in spite of the fact that he mainly worked at Faithfield Holistic Hospital and only taught two classes at FSUni. Everybody was interested in his nutrition research and pressed him to write about his findings and serve on curriculum-design committees. He was proud of being a faculty member in an institution so dedicated to survival and well-being, but he also loved his trailblazing work at Faithfield Holistic Hospital.

So, Steve, who had tried all his life to avoid the limelight, was anxious and not quite sure how to handle his fame, although he was delighted to be appreciated. Surely he was glad that people were learning how to live healthy, sustainable lives, and considered it his duty to assist them, but he loved his research and knew that becoming a public figure would decrease the precious time he would have to dedicate to his research.

It was a pleasant and warm spring evening two months following the latest disaster. The FSUni campus sprang to life. Youthful energy, laughter, and small talk filled the air. Birds tweeted happily, announcing that life was good in spite of the disasters. Steve left the classroom with the single thought of getting home as soon as possible. But he could not resist the smell of the flowers and the sense of hope invoked by the dry, warm wind. *I am too tired to drive home now. Why don't I get a good cup of coffee in the cafeteria and a piece of pastry to go with it?* Steve smiled at his sudden need to indulge, acknowledging that after Charlotte had left and rented a room at Vanessa's, his meals, although very nutritious, had been very boring.

"Hey, Steve, glad to see you, busy guy! I have been wanting to talk with you for a long time, but you have always been either in class, the lab, or a meeting."

Steve turned her way, unable to suppress his wide grin and shy blushing. "Excited to see you, Daphne! I apologize for being too busy to meet my neighbor, but it's all for a good cause. What's up?"

"Why don't we talk about it over a cup of coffee? I hope you are not on your way to a class or meeting."

"I am on my way to the cafeteria as well," he replied, admiring her athletic figure, her beautiful, delicate pale face, her deep blue eyes, and her carefully combed long blonde hair. *She is so gorgeous and successful and nonetheless so friendly,* he thought.

At the cafeteria, they tried to find a quiet table as far as possible from a vocal group of students.

"I remember that you mentioned during the Oasis teleconference that you study horticulture here, on top of your acting career. Is that what brought you to campus so late in the evening?"

"Glad you remember that. I am sure you noticed that I had taken your nutrition class. It was a great class, and I got an A. Thank you for teaching it."

Steve squeezed his shoulders together, clasped his hands, and stayed mum. Of course, he'd had no clue. Daphne was quick to rescue him. "I am in a combined program of horticulture, nutrition, and film/broadcasting studies. My vision has been to start producing and broadcasting programs to inform the entire population about horticulture, nutrition, and health issues. And guess what! The Film and Broadcasting Department agreed to support the program. I am so excited! And here is where you come in to the picture. I want you to be on the board of the program and also be a guest star."

Oh my God, he thought, *another duty. But how can I say no to her?*

"Look, Daphne, I would like to help you, but I am so busy! I will probably be able to squeeze in a couple of appearances, but I cannot be deeply involved in the programming."

"Steve, I appreciate your devotion to your research. But what benefit would come of it if you do not share it with the broader population?! Now is the time to make a difference. Just imagine how the information the program provides will affect the survival, health, and quality of life of millions. Tomorrow is the first board meeting at 6:00 p.m. I expect you to be there!"

Steve agreed with a big sigh, deploring the foiling of his plan to go home from the hospital and catch up on his research work.

"Well, I understand that you prefer the company of your plants over people, but I think you should cheer up and meet new people now that you are single again."

Steve's voice was cold, even hostile, when he responded: "Daphne, I have been single all along. I have never thought about my relationship with Charlotte as a lasting one and, as you very well know, neither did she. She is an excellent nurse and a pleasant companion, but not very trustworthy. And I don't need social counseling."

Daphne murmured: "I am sorry, Steve. It was not my place to meddle in your private life. I have tremendous respect for you and your work. My intentions were good. I thought I had a chance to convince you to become more involved socially. … I am sorry if I angered you. It's late, and we are both tired. Let's start over tomorrow. We have important work to do."

As she rose from her chair, Steve noticed that the noisy group of students had become quiet and were looking at them, pointing their fingers in Steve's direction. One student approached their table hesitantly.

"Dr. Grisham, I am Marc North. I attended your horticulture class today and have never been so inspired. I am mostly interested in your herbal studies and want to learn more from you. I know that you have no funds to hire an assistant, so I am willing to help you for free if you promise to teach me."

"I can use some help in my research. Can we discuss it further tomorrow evening? I have a meeting on campus and can see you afterward in my office, I guess around 8:00 p.m."

"I will be there," Marc responded, clapping his hands. Then he hurriedly returned to his friends to tell them the good news.

"As I told you, we all need you. You are an inspiration," said Daphne, her voice choked with tears. She left.

Steve looked at the students, and for the first time he felt the weight of great responsibility. He knew that now that the university had lost some of its older, experienced faculty, there was nobody better them him to integrate his areas of interests and design a new curriculum that supports sustainable living. This reluctant hero knew deep down inside that Daphne was right, although he'd rather she had not alluded to the relationship between him and Charlotte. He also realized that he could not accomplish his goals by himself and would need help. Marc had shown him the way. *I should ask for help,* he thought. His guts were quivering. Could he meet all these people's expectations?

◆◆◆◆◆

Steve was determined to become more sociable and carve some time out of his busy schedule to visit the café, meet his neighbors, and hopefully run into Daphne and continue where they had left off at FSUni. So far, Daphne was a no-show, and although he had met her in the board meetings and even discussed appearing on her show, their conversation was very businesslike.

In the absence of Daphne, he watched his neighbors, noticing how two months with no disaster had resulted in more laughter and jokes in the cafeteria and more interest in group activities in the classrooms, which were filled as soon as school ended. He even visited the basement and participated in a much-needed workout. He plunged into the pool, where singles and family were frolicking in the water or doing laps, convincing himself that as a physician, he should be an example of a healthy lifestyle beyond the nutrition part. He had started a swimming regimen and noticed how much more energized he'd become. Before showering at home, he checked his abs, hoping to see a somewhat more toned body reflected in the mirror.

Still, the memory of the past years was traumatic enough to allow complacency to settle in. He could still remember the terrible storms resulting in numerous wounded and maimed people who filled Faithfield's hospitals above capacity. Nor could he forget the last OD attack, when he'd faced the senseless cruelty that had caused so much death and suffering. He knew that it is not the end of it, but the news about East was sparse. He did not know what to expect.

Although he pretty much knew what each of the council members was going to say, he was looking forward to Friday night, when the first formal residents' meeting would take place. He was hoping to finally meet Daphne and enjoy the nice communal dinner that preceded the meeting.

On Friday he returned home as early as he could. He looked through his old clothes and selected his relatively new light brown pants and patterned shirt, which he believed would make him look attractive. Then he looked at himself in the mirror, combed his hair again, and left. He arrived early. Not seeing Daphne, he engaged himself in conversation with a group of neighbors.

Finally, he saw her entering. She took a seat. He hurried to seize the empty chair beside her. Trying to hide his emotions, he asked her if she minded. She smiled and reassured him that she was glad to see him. They had a nice talk during dinner.

The meeting went as he expected. After a short introduction by Stanly, each council member reported achievements and successes. Sustainit had added to its payroll Vanessa as treasurer, and the two social workers who had lost their jobs. The company branched out into the production of greenhouses and took pride in helping to restore Faithville homes damaged by the storm and the bombing.

Laura, the education coordinator, reported that she and the other teachers had organized the curriculum for the three preschoolers and six elementary schoolchildren of the community. The children were happy and were showing considerable progress. The group of teachers had designed several projects, some experimentally, involving children of multiple ages, with the older children teaching the younger children and with students of all ages working on projects together. With the help of the parents and some donations from the store owner and Stanly, the teachers had purchased computers, signed up for online resources, and even obtained some books for the small library. They had also developed an electronic library of free materials and purchased programs and worksheets. "We now have a full homeschooling program for preschool to grade twelve. This means that the two older children, currently studying in town, will be able to receive education on-site in the event of hazardous situations." She concluded by inviting all the adults in the community to contribute to the youngsters' education by sharing their experience and knowledge with the children. All nodded in agreement.

"I hope they will not ask me to teach kindergarten nutrition," said Steve jokingly to Daphne.

"Steve, it's about time that you come down from the summit of Olympus. Whether or not we have children, we need to support our local school. I volunteered to help one day, and was impressed to see happy kids running around, enjoying tasty healthy meals cooked in the kitchen, and learning in classrooms adorned with their pictures and projects."

Steve shrugged. "Maybe I need to have children to appreciate it," he said, surprised by his own boldness. Daphne smiled mischievously. He saw the notes Daphne had brought with her and wondered when it would be her turn to speak. Looking around, he smiled to Liz, noticing that she and her two teenage boys were in attendance, but her husband was not there.

Next was Fred, who started as usual by boasting about his ingenuity to get everything he needed. With Vanessa at his side, he unveiled a plan to develop the store into a marketing venue for Oasis goods. "Anyone who wants to sell excess food, either fresh produce or preserves, please come and talk to me. I will find a way to sell it either to other residents, if there is a demand, or to buyers outside Oasis. This applies to milk products as well." He encouraged everybody to come up with suggestions.

"Great job, Fred. We all admire what you have accomplished, and we love our community store. Next, we will hear from Vanessa and then from Daphne," declared Stanly.

Vanessa reported that the financial state of affairs was very good, especially because of the revenue received from the sale of one of the lots owned by the community to a future resident and the sale of surplus produce grown in the community greenhouse.

Ralph, the banker, cut her short. "Are we becoming a commune?" he asked, shaking his head in disbelief. With a shaking voice, he added. "Is the next move sharing all our wealth?"

"Relax, Ralph. We are becoming a community, not a commune. Nobody is going to nationalize your bank, or should I say Oasianalize your bank," responded Stanly. All laughed heartily. "Seriously, being a community means that we do share some wealth, like the community center, and that we are concerned about the well-being of the community as a whole and each member of the community. So yes, we have some communal capital, but not all the capital is shared."

"Okay, I might have overreacted," he answered, noticing that all seemed to agree with Stanly's stance.

Finally, Daphne stood up. "I cannot report glorious achievements as the former presenters have done. But I worked with, among others, our own Dr. Steve Grisham to develop a broadcast educational program that benefits everybody in our viewing area, including Oasis. The teachers told me that they downloaded the episodes and used them to teach our schoolchildren basic horticulture and nutrition. The program has received rave reviews from viewers from all walks of life. I am aware that we need to do more internally, but right now I have in mind two projects: directing a show with the schoolchildren, possibly adults too, and preparing Thanksgiving celebration three months from now. I am not sure if we want to pay for entertainers or speakers to come here, but I am open to suggestions."

Steve was pleased that she had mentioned him and that his teaching would be used for grade school after all.

Clara expressed her wish to add more spirituality to the

community life, not necessarily religion, although she was glad to see people using the center for religious prayers and ceremonies. She mentioned meditation, her shamanic journeying group, and other ways to connect with the Divine, such as reading Akashic records, which she would be glad to teach if there was interest. Some eyebrows were raised when Clara spoke. People looked at each other shrugging and grimacing.

Before anybody responded, Daphne jumped in. "Thanks, Clara. It's an excellent idea. I know we have many talents here, artists, musicians, and yes, spiritual teachers. I suggest that anybody who wants to create a new interest group should send a message to everyone describing briefly what the group is about and asking who is interested. Then, the organizer will contact those interested and find the time when we all can meet. Thankfully, our center provides comfortable meeting areas. I would love to be in your group, Clara. Please count me in."

Daphne's last sentence was masked by quick steps and loud voices approaching the meeting area from the entrance door. All heads turned as two men dressed in army fatigues entered the room. "Sorry to interrupt your meeting," said the taller guy. We are from the state's intelligence administration. We detected signals from Oasis contacting East and West and providing information about our army's moves. We located the communication device at the Tarvers' residence and caught Bill communicating with our enemy. He is now in custody." Clara sent a quick questioning look to Rudolph, the communicator to whom she expressed her suspicion a few months earlier, but he looked the other way.

"It's impossible! It must be a mistake," exclaimed Liz, Bill's wife. "He is a good man working hard to provide for his family and our community." She ran outside, followed by some curious residents, and saw her husband in shackles. "Billy, tell me that this is a mistake!" His gaze was cold, and he said nothing.

"Sorry to hurt you, madam! We have no proof that you knew about it." Pulling a device from his bag, the man said to Liz, "This is the transmitter. Have you ever seen it?"

She trembled and shook her head, sobbing. The two men turned around, entered their pickup, and vanished with Bill. Rudolph, who had been uncharacteristically quiet during the entire meeting, turned to Liz. "We are all shocked and sorry. We love you and your children and appreciate your contribution to our community. Your butter and cheeses are irreplaceable. We are going to help you and the children. As Stanly said before, we are a caring community."

Steve and Daphne approached Liz and hugged her, promising to help.

The meeting ended on a somber note. People hurried to leave.

"Why can't we have one quiet, joyous evening without surprises?" Steve sighed as he accompanied Daphne to her home. At her doorstep, he kept talking until she smiled and invited him in for a cup of coffee.

CHAPTER 6

CALLAHAN'S ESCAPE

James Callahan struggled to keep his eyes open. He had been unable to obtain a stealth car and had not dared using the automatic driver, which might have revealed his location. He had been driving almost nonstop for fifteen hours and finally had reached Austin, the city of his alma mater. Although it had changed a lot since his graduation twenty-eight years ago, he felt a warm sense of familiarity as he navigated his way to the west side of the town. He had not contacted his old friend Tom Vargas for a long time, having been afraid to reveal any contacts outside OD-controlled territory. Hoping for the best, he knew he should have made a plan B. Only, there was no plan B. If Tom declined to help, Callahan would be on his own.

It was early morning. Callahan noticed that the traffic was uncharacteristically light compared to what he remembered of Austin's heyday. *Maybe people travel less nowadays due to the new circumstances,* he mused, wondering whether or not the city was still creative and exuberant as he remembered it. The homes, somewhat hidden by the old oaks and mighty cedars, were welcoming but seemed to hide some dark secrets. *I am too tired, and hallucinating,* he thought. Taking a deep breath, Callahan called his friend's old number, hoping that it had not changed and that the communications system still worked.

"Hello," whispered a raspy, suspicious voice. Callahan was tremendously relieved when he heard the distinct voice of his friend Tom.

"Tom, is that you? Hi, buddy, it's Jim, Jim Callahan. I am in town, and I gotta see ya."

Silence. "Jimmy, is it really you? Long time, no see. How did you pop up in Austin?"

"Look, Tom, I know I have not contacted you for a long time. I will tell you everything when I see you. But I have got to see you right away."

A few moments of silence ensued. Finally, he heard Tom's hesitant voice.

"Please come over. I hope you still remember the way. Sorry I am not that enthusiastic about meeting a good old friend. We heard terrible things about East. We need to talk before I determine what I can do for you. I cannot put my family at risk."

"I fully understand. Maybe we should not meet at your home."

"I am by myself. Everybody else has already left for work or school. We need to talk before they come back."

Fifteen minutes later Tom opened the door and embraced Callahan. "Good Lord, you look terrible!" he exclaimed.

"I am exhausted. I have driven almost nonstop for about sixteen hours. Just escaped from East. I don't think the OD followed me after I crossed the Mississippi, but if they locate me, they will shoot me. I need your help. If you tell me to leave, I will understand, but first, can I get something to eat? I am starving."

Tom fetched some food and put it on the table. Then he poured some coffee from the pot.

"Jimmy, I don't think they followed your either, but I will be honest with you. We all know that you worked for the OD, and heard horrific stories about their atrocities. So, pardon my disbelief. Why should I believe that you have escaped? And how could you escape their lines? The electronic control of their territory is known for its superb quality. And where are Sophie and Jacob anyway?"

Callahan was no longer sure that calling Tom was a good idea, but it was too late—he had already told him that he had run away from the OD. Deep down inside, he knew that he should have disappeared in Central like Sophie. Now he was too tired to drive any further and was practically at Tom's mercy. All that was left to do was to try to paint himself as a person who had done his best for the uprooted suffering refugees, within the OD's restrictions. He described Sophie's escape, saying that it had caused the OD to sever all their contracts with him, and discussed his decision to move south, mentioning that OD control there was less tight. He hoped that this would help convince Tom that he was not an OD spy.

Callahan continued telling Tom about his decision to escape as soon as was feasible, especially after the OD had started executing some of their own people for treason. Callahan said he was sure that he would be next. Then, to calm Tom's suspicion about his easy escape, he told him about the numerous business trips he'd taken to Florida before he decided to escape and how during the last trip he had left his bugged car in a used-car shop and bought a van instead. He bragged about smashing his bugged phone to pieces, getting a wig, changing his attire to look like a local, and getting some false papers just in case.

"I could not even recognize myself when I looked in the mirror," he said, smiling. "Since they only follow people on their list, they did not have a reason to follow me until they noticed my disappearance. So, I did not have a problem when crossing the border."

"Go to sleep now. I asked my wife to pick up the children from school and then go to her sister's. I need to leave now, but I will return home before my wife and children. When you wake up, I want you to tell our people what you have just said to me." Callahan was too tired to think about what Tom meant by "our people." Once he was settled in the guest room, he fell into a deep sleep.

———— ◆◆◆◆◆ ————

Callahan woke up, jumping from his bed in fear. "Where am I?" The last day's events ran through his mind in fast-forward mode. The room was dark. Looking through the window, he saw the light in the neighbors' homes. *Is it possible that I have slept through the entire day?* He located the light switch in his room, turned it on, walked into the adjacent bathroom, jumped in the shower, and for a long time allowed his body to enjoy the hot water. Then, he put on some clean clothes, left his room, and stepped into the living room. The entire house was dark and silent. *Where is everybody?* In spite of the heat wave, Callahan was shivering uncontrollably. *Could Tom have betrayed me? Is he in trouble for attempting to help me?* Since he did not have any weapon, he figured that the darkness was his best defense. *I should turn the lights off in my room and wait in the garden,* he thought. Then he turned around.

He felt a sharp blow on his head. Before passing out, he heard a crackling noise getting louder. "Helicopter!"

Tom Vargas drove home with two men and a woman, his friends from Texas Intelligence Services. He'd meant to return home much earlier, but he was held up in the office taking care of some issues. As he approached the driveway, his headlights leaped over the elongated cracks in the cement's surface. He stopped the car abruptly and ran up to his house. The front door was unlocked, and the entire home was dark. He called James's name, although deep down inside he knew that Callahan was no longer there. His companions followed him inside.

"Where is your famous refugee?" asked Chen. "Apparently, he did not appreciate your hospitality and found a better place to stay."

Tom ignored the irony in Chen's voice. "He could not have gotten too far, given that his car is still parked here … unless he was kidnapped."

"So, either the Illuminati got him after all, or he got in touch with their agents here and made it look like a kidnapping."

Tom, knowing right then that there was a spy in the agency, decided to keep his ideas of the other possibility to himself. These three companions were the only ones who knew about Callahan. So who was it: Chen? Vera? Juan?

A knock on the door was followed by the peeping head of his neighbor across the street. Her high feminine voice shrieked in pretentious concern: "Sorry to interrupt, Tom. I just wanted to make sure you are okay. Any idea why a helicopter landed in your driveway? And who did they pick up?"

"Helicopter? Really? I have no idea what are you talking about! Glad you told me about the helicopter. That explains the cracks in the driveway. Luckily Lorna and the kids are at her sister's. It would have scared them to death. I am fine. I will try to find out what a helicopter was doing on my driveway. Oh, by the way, when did the helicopter land?"

She looked suspiciously at Chen, Juan, and Vera, and murmured, "Glad you are okay. It happened about half an hour ago. Let me know if there is something else I can do to help." After closing the door, she disappeared.

"How could the Illuminati operate a helicopter within Texas?" asked Chen.

Tom thought about all the obstacles for promotion he had faced within the agency, now seemingly intentional, and felt icicles running through his veins. Knowing now that the agency had been infiltrated by spies, he thought that if he was not careful, he and his family would be in jeopardy.

He clicked on a number on his phone and typed a message: "Did you see a helicopter flying over Lakeway around 6:00 p.m.?" The answer came rapidly.

"They spotted a helicopter belonging to the coast guard that was on duty in the area and now is heading west," he told Chen, Juan, and Vera.

"Does not sound like the Illuminati to me," said Vera. Oppressive silence ensued.

Finally, the meek, hesitant voice of Tom uttered, "They are trying to fool us. Who else could have done it?"

-------- ·✦✦✦✦✦· --------

James Callahan opened his eyes. The small darkened room had a few items of furniture, had no decorations, and looked unfamiliar. *Am I still dreaming?* As he was rubbing his eyes, the stark truth started sinking in. He remembered the long drive from Florida to Austin and meeting his good friend Tom Vargas. "Ouch!" Touching his head, he felt a wet swollen spot and sharp pain. He realized that somebody had hit him and probably taken him away. His mind started working diligently, sorting things out and creating possible scenarios of what might have happened. Had he underestimated the OD? Had Vargas or somebody in his group betrayed him? He got up and tried to open the door. The door was locked. *I am a prisoner,* he realized. The small window above eye level did not reveal much about the surroundings. He felt famished and thirsty. *Is this the end of the line?*

He heard quiet steps approaching the room. Without anyone knocking, the door opened wide. Two Chinese figures appeared, smiling in reassurance.

"Where am I? How did I get here? Who are you?" he asked angrily.

The older of the two, who looked quite authoritative, responded, "You are in California, having been summoned by California's government. We need you to build communities like the ones you built in several locations, including the three in California. We do not want the Illuminati government to know that you are here, so we are going to change your identity. You are going to be fine as long as you cooperate with our government. Sorry for the painful way we kidnapped you; it was necessary. Is there something you need right now?"

"How about something to eat and drink?"

A young beautiful Chinese woman entered the room, carrying a tray with a bowl of steaming wonton soup, a plate of beef and broccoli, a bowl of rice, and some dumplings, all smelling delicious. A chilled bottle of Coke accompanied the meal. She placed the tray on the small table adjacent to Callahan's bed, bowed slightly, and left. Aware of being watched, Callahan fought the urge to devour the food. He forced himself to chew very slowly. While eating, he figured that his best strategy right now was to cooperate. If they had the means to find him in Texas, an operation that the OD were not capable of, they would surely find him should he escape again. Being a guy who had always landed on his feet, Callahan tried to look at the situation with a bit of humor. *At least I will get to compare the OD and the Chinese and determine who is better.* A full stomach and the reassurance that he was not in any immediate danger improved his mood.

"As you know, building communities is my passion, and I am glad to help with any survival project. You could have just asked."

"We are not as stupid as your friends in East, so please don't treat us as such," responded the older Chinese man in a rough voice. "You will work for the government-supported company Ecological Builders. They are going to finance several projects across the state, and you are going to assist with the planning and execution. They will pay you for your services and take care of your rent and utility bills. I arranged for you to meet Mr. Wei, the company CEO, this afternoon. We are leaving now!" Pointing toward the younger man, he added, "Chen will be your driver and guide."

They sure do not waste their time, he thought, getting up and following the two men.

Callahan reclined in the back seat. Looking out the window, he observed the passing homes and fields, enjoying the pleasantly sunny California day. It had been three years since he last visited. He wondered to what extent the numerous earthquakes along the San Andreas Fault, the rising of the sea level, and the severe storms that had killed or displaced millions had ravaged the state. To his astonishment, he could not see any of such damage.

The blinding sunrays penetrating from the driver's side implied that they were going north. But from where to where? He was unconscious when they'd landed in California, and none of the places they drove by now looked familiar. He figured that since there were no significant signs of devastation, they were probably far away from both the Pacific Ocean and the San Andreas Fault. His best guess at this point, given the flatness of the land, was that they were somewhere in the Central Valley. The road sign rushing toward them read Merced. He was pleased that his guess had turned out to be right. *We probably landed in Fresno,* he inferred.

Forty-five minutes after they'd left, they entered a complex of square gray buildings lacking any landscaping, which stood in sharp contrast to the lush vegetation he'd seen during the trip. Chen led him to a stern, colorless office displaying conspicuous pictures of California's governor Wang and China's president. The man at the desk stood up and greeted them.

"Delun Wei, Ecological Builders CEO. I am glad to meet you, Mr. Callahan. I have heard a lot about you, and I hope you will meet our expectations. I am sure that you are exhausted, so you will start working tomorrow at 8:00 a.m. Please report to me. You will rest this afternoon. We found you a lovely apartment within a short walking distance from the office. Your belongings, including your computer, are already there. We purchased some food and other necessities for you. There is a small store nearby if you need anything else. Do not leave town. See you tomorrow."

The small apartment greeted Callahan with a huge communications screen that bespoke government propaganda. After the initial shock, Callahan noticed the blue sofa and brown oak table. A glimpse at the small kitchenette revealed that it had all the necessities. Entering the bedroom, he saw his suitcase on the floor. A full-size bed, all made up and ready to climb into, a closet against the perpendicular wall, and a small desk and a bookcase completed the basic furniture provided. His computer was on top of the desk. "Surely they copied everything they needed from the computer, but did they have the courtesy to keep the suitcase intact?" He opened it swiftly. All his belongings seemed to be intact, but some documents were gone.

As promised, the fridge and pantry had enough food for the meantime, but he was not hungry. Instead of eating, he turned on the communication device, hoping to learn something about the new reality in California. He watched interviews with white Californians praising the Chinese government for its swift assistance to the survivors of the earthquakes and the coastal flooding, and mentioning how the Chinese government had resettled them and helped them to find jobs and support themselves. The news told horrible stories about the OD's rule in the East but was mum about Central. Callahan learned that Russia had regained control of the countries previously under control of the Soviet Union and that it was currently dictating the politics of the Middle East as well. He wondered whether or not he could trust these sources. China was portrayed as a benevolent country helping Africa, East Asia, and the western United States to cope with the multitude of disasters that had hit them, while the local governments have done nothing. All China asked in return was to allow Chinese immigrants to settle peacefully in those countries.

Well, I assume my job would be to build communities for these newcomers, and given that the Chinese have bought a lot land over the last forty years, they even don't have to dislocate existing residents. He flipped stations and found himself watching the Movie Channel. The choices of languages were English, Spanish, and Chinese. *I wonder what Hollywood is up to these days?* he contemplated.

He chose the English language. The selection included mostly old movies that preceded 2050, the beginning of the severe disasters across the world. After some searching, he found one newer movie from 2056. The producer, New Reality Movies, and the names of the Chinese director and the multiethnic cast were unfamiliar to him. The story was about the eternal triangle of a white man and a Chinese man working in an automobile factory who fell for the same beautiful female Chinese coworker. The dialogue included some clichés and some lecturing about the Chinese worldview and philosophy. But the movie was also blessed with a few hilarious situations of chasing and misunderstanding that made the movie funny, though far from inspiring.

Before going to bed, Callahan stumbled upon a program called *Citizen Complaints*. There were some predictable complaints about the quality of the water, blackouts, and other malfunctions, which the government representative tried patiently to resolve. But then somebody complained about Chinese immigration. The answer was determined and lengthy, but the essence of it was: "You white people have the audacity to complain? We have respected the indigenous people of the land, the Native Americans, and haven't touched the small reservations you have left them. But you have no more right to be here than we do. You fled from Europe when you needed shelter, and now we have done the same. Moreover, you agreed to naturalize us in exchange for the help provided to you by our government. We have the world's greatest density of population. Our people need new locations to live, and we are finding them across the world. Unlike you, we do not try to eliminate the existing population. We work with it and support it."

The following morning, Callahan went to work. As he expected, he got involved in designing a new community for Chinese newcomers not far away. The team members were ethnically diverse, and they listened to his suggestions with utmost attention. He was humbled, given that now he was Gene Kerrigan, a salt-and-pepper-bearded engineer and former employee of California Development. Nobody connected him with the energetic, suave, black-haired CEO who had built Glamor, Charisma, and Gorgeous. He performed professionally, but his previous enthusiasm was gone.

Attempting to find out as much as possible about what was

happening, Callahan tried to befriend as many coworkers and neighbors as possible and encouraged them to tell him their stories, while trying to say the least possible about himself. He started getting used to the new normal and his new routine, seeing no way out. Callahan-turned-Kerrigan realized that the Chinese propaganda was exaggerated but not untrue. People were thankful for the Chinese help and accepted the new immigrants as a necessary evil. However, they also expressed concern that in time the newcomers would try to dominate the non-Chinese with the help of the existing Asian population.

The holidays approached. James felt his loneliness more than ever. He, as had all Ecological Builders professional employees, received an invitation from Delun Wei and his wife, Sonya, to attend a party at their beautiful suburban home. He had heard a lot of stories about Wei's beautiful white wife and was curious to see her in the flesh.

Full of anticipation, he knocked on the door. Delun Wei opened it.

"Good evening, Gene. Glad to see you! Please meet my wife, Sonya."

He paled, leaving his hand midway in the air between him and Wei's wife. Seeing the look of terror and pleading on Sonya's face, he took a deep breath.

"Gene Kerrigan. Glad to meet you, madam."

"Do you two know each other?" asked the CEO, whose sharp eye had not missed the tense exchange.

"Yes, we do, sir. It's an old story."

Callahan knew that he had better confirm his boss's suspicions, because the truth was quite evident. Another employee showed up, and Callahan slipped away to the festive living room. Being a tough guy who had undergone many challenges, he knew how to control his feelings, but nothing had prepared him for what had just happened.

At least I know she is alive. Jacob is not around, but I hope that our son is well.

He did his best to look jolly so as to avoid further suspicion, thinking of when it would be appropriate to leave. It turned out he was glad he had not left too early. As people got crowded around the abundantly laid table, he felt something pushed into his pocket. Fifteen minutes later, in the privacy of the bathroom, he read the note:

> Jacob, now Jerome Kline, is okay. You can find him at the local university. I did not have another choice. You are one of my past boyfriends. I have divorced you and will mail you your copy of the legal papers.
>
> S.

He tore the paper into small pieces, threw the pieces into the bowl, and flushed the toilet. Then he returned to the living room. When he saw a group of people leaving, he thanked both hosts and joined the exiting guests.

In the privacy of his little apartment, lying on his bed, Callahan was trying to digest the new reality. *It's all over.* He wanted to scream. Although he had tried to convince himself that he would never see Sophie and Jacob again, he had held a stubborn hope that one day he would find them and try to do better this time. Now, he doubted that she'd even loved him when she left. He felt betrayed twice.

A week later, the letter with the divorce documents arrived in the mail, with an unknown sender's return address. The documents had been issued about three weeks after Sophie had escaped. *She could not wait to get rid of me,* he thought bitterly.

CHAPTER 7

THE PLAGUE

Steve sat in his car in the North Faithfield supermarket's parking lot, ready to buy some necessities for the weekend. He was thinking about his blossoming relationship with Daphne, smiling as he pictured himself holding her warmly in his arms. His longing for Daphne was interrupted by a sharp sense that a woman like her would never fall in love with an uninspiring guy like him. As he attempted to clear his mind of these disturbing thoughts, he raised his eyes and saw a sign for a big furniture sale at a store next to the supermarket. He felt a strong urge to buy new furniture for the living, guest, and dining rooms, knowing he couldn't invite Daphne to his barren home. He remembered the warmth he had felt when he visited her home and thought of the stark difference between the ambiance of the two houses. Forgetting his intention to buy some food items, he left his car and walked to the furniture store. He stepped in hesitantly.

The store owner recognized him immediately as one of the guests at Daphne's shows and welcomed him warmly. "Thanks for stopping by, Dr. Grisham. How can I help you?"

"I ... I need some furniture for my living and dining room. I postponed it for so long. ... I needed the money for my lab and research. I saw that you are having a sale and thought that maybe I could find something I can afford."

The owner could not hide his surprise about Steve's apologetic tone and his apparent lack of means to buy. "Don't worry, Dr.

Grisham. I will give you a good price!" he said, anticipating how he would tell his wife and friends about meeting the famous Dr. Grisham.

Steve looked around. The selection was limited, but he knew that the same would apply to every furniture warehouse in town these days. Steve did find some items that he liked and figured out the price in his mind. *Oh my God, that's all my savings!* he thought.

"How much?"

"I have promised you a good price. The prices are already reduced, but I will take 20 percent off and sell everything you've picked out for three thousand dollars.

"This is the last price," he added, noticing the hesitation in Steve's face.

"Including delivery?"

"I will deliver it to your residence myself," he answered. He had not meant that the price included delivery, but he was curious enough to see Dr. Grisham's home to risk the transaction.

"When can you deliver it?"

"Tonight, after I close."

Forgetting his intention to visit the supermarket, Steve drove home thinking that he would have to at least clean the house up a bit, and organize his books, prints, and notes that were spread over every surface.

A few hours later, the big truck rolled up. Hearing the noise, Steve went out to greet the owner. He noticed many curious faces watching the new arrival with interest.

That's what you get for living in a small community, he thought. *No privacy and no secrets.* He just waved to his neighbors.

That evening Steve enjoyed the new furniture. He even remembered that he had a box with some pictures and other decorations. After finding it, he got busy hanging and arranging things. He had good aesthetic sense, only aesthetics had never been a priority before. *Nice. It looks much better, and to be honest, it feels great as well. I will get the research instrument next month,* he thought.

The telephone rang. "Dr. Grisham, this is Nurse Betty from Faithfield Holistic Hospital. We have two patients with an unidentifiable disease. We called Blessed Health Hospital, and they had one patient who died and at least one more patient with the same symptoms. I think you should come and check it out."

"I will be there shortly."

Then another phone call came in. "Hi, Steve. It's Daphne! I hope you have not forgotten our date tonight. I can't wait to see your new furniture. Everybody in Oasis is talking about it after the truck rolled into your driveway."

"Sorry, Daphne. Of course I didn't forget. But I just got a call from Faithfield Holistic about an unidentifiable disease that affected two of our patients, and it appears that somebody in Blessed Health has died from it. If we are facing an epidemic of some sort, we need to know as soon as possible, figure out what the disease is, and take precautions. I am leaving for the hospital right now. I planned to call you on my way."

"Oh, that is terrible! I trust that you can help. Please call me when you can."

"I will, Daphne, but it might not be until tomorrow. Good night. I love you."

He hung up the phone and left his house. He was driving to Faithville, ignoring the traffic around him, letting his faithful car travel the well-known route. Trembling, he held the wheel tight, his thoughts racing and imagining the most horrific scenarios. He had always dreaded a breakout following a major disaster and was thankful that no major lethal disease had spread in the area so far. He'd known that one day it would happen, and had dedicated his life to being able to avert a health disaster. That day was now, and he would need all his ingenuity to find a cure. *Will I be able to do it? Is everything I have done sufficient?* Forgetting his fatigue and his anticipation to show Daphne his new furniture, he parked his car and ran into the hospital.

A nurse led him to a section on the third floor dedicated to existing and potential cases. On the way, she told him that the patients looked as if they were having panic attacks. They were shaking uncontrollably, sweating, and having a hard time breathing, and one of them kept vomiting.

When they reached the third floor, Steve saw his dear friend Dr. Gary Coleman.

"Steve, it looks like a panic attack, but no known treatment has worked. The symptoms will not subside. The patients are incoherent and are incapable of describing what they feel. I have already contacted the health secretary in Denver. He said that they have received several similar reports from different locations that are far away from each other. So far, nobody has discovered the source of the disorder, whether or not there is a common cause for all the breakouts, or how to cure it. There are three reports of death, including the one in Faithfield."

"Gary, what tests have you performed?"

"The patients are running a high fever, between 102°F and 104°F, and their pulse is very high, around 120. That could be the result of the shaking. Blood tests show a high level of protein. The rest is normal. We sent some samples for genetic analysis to see if there is any viral or bacterial infection. The results are not back yet, but I doubt that they will discover something. I gave the patients an antiviral–antibacterial combo, but so far there is no improvement. I am afraid to stick a needle into them because of the shaking. It was a fight to draw the blood samples. The patient's death at Blessed Health occurred after they had sedated him, so we need to be cautious."

Steve looked at the three patients through the glass of their closed ward and was stunned by the fierce fear in their eyes. They were tied to the bed for their own safety and for the safety of the hazmat-suited nurse who attended them. Steve tried to communicate with them via the intercom, to no avail.

"Did you talk with family members?"

"Yes," responded Dr. Coleman. "I have just spoken with Bob's wife. She arrived after we called you and told us that it started all of a sudden and that she had not noticed anything abnormal beforehand. She had to go back to take care of their kids. All the other people involved with the patients told the same story. They had not noticed anything suspicious until it broke, and then they shoved the patient into the car and drove to the hospital."

"If there were only one patient, I would think it is some psychological disorder, but five in Faithfield and more across the country ... Even if it is related to the trauma of the last disasters, something should have triggered it. We have not had a major climate-related issue for four months. We need to look into changes in the quality of air, food, and water, and for any unusual bacterium or virus," contemplated Steve.

"The state has started to look into it. We are going to create a Faithfield interdisciplinary team of physicians and university professors to investigate. I suggested that you represent our hospital. They will contact you with details about the first meeting. I know that you are busy, Steve, and that you are worried, like all of us are, about a cure, but don't even think about refusing this request. We have to get to the root of the problem, and you are the best we have. Go home now and get some rest tonight and tomorrow. We will do our best here. Sorry for dragging you here, but you had to see it to believe it. You have a shift on Sunday, right?"

"Yeah, I will be here before Sunday if I come up with an idea. And let me know if something shows up in the tests."

"Will do. I will leave instructions with the nurses to keep you posted. And knowing you, you will probably call every two hours to find out. Get some rest, buddy; you will need it."

Steve drove on the poorly lit road, calling Daphne on his way home.

"Daphne, it is Steve. I am on my way back home. Can I stop by?"

"Please do, dear. And drive carefully. You sound very upset!"

He parked the car in the garage and went into Daphne's home. He entered without knocking and headed to the living room. Steve hugged Daphne and saw a full glass of wine and some refreshments waiting for him at the table. He gulped the wine and immediately felt a pleasant dizziness.

"Daphne, I have never seen a patient with such a dreadful facial expression. All three looked as if the devil were chasing them. They are completely uncommunicative, so we do not know for sure what is going on with them. And the shaking and sweat. ... None of the tests so far have come up with a possible cause. Excessive sedation might kill them. One patient in Blessed Health has already died. They called me about two cases, and by the time I got there, I found three. I feel so helpless. ... We need to figure something out."

"You are exhausted, Steve; you cannot find out anything right now."

She embraced him and led him to the bedroom. He succumbed to the fatigue and fell asleep, clothes on, right away. Daphne covered him gently with a blanket and turned the lights off. Tortured by nightmares, Steve was moving violently and screaming during his sleep. When he finally woke up early in the morning, he grabbed the extra clothes bag he had carried in from his car and took a shower. Stepping into the kitchen, he saw Daphne sitting at the table, all set for breakfast, and watching the news. He joined her. As they were eating, she looked at her watch and said, "We have to hurry. We need to be at Clara's at nine o'clock for a shamanic drumming session."

"We? Daphne, give me a break! I have too much work to do today and do not have time for this ..." He stopped there, swallowing the word *nonsense*. "I do want to spend as much as time as I can with you, but I am not doing that. How about lunch later, say, around one o'clock?"

"Steve, I have never told you what to do, but now I insist. Let yourself be surprised. It might help your cause more than you think. As the saying goes, extraordinary times call for extraordinary measures."

"How long will it take?" he asked, thinking that this was the second time in twenty-four hours that somebody has told him he cannot refuse to do something. He contemplated how to be better at saying no, knowing very well he could not say no to Daphne.

"Only about two hours. I will prepare lunch and supper if you wish so that you can dedicate the rest of the day to your work. Let's go."

Reluctantly, he got up. Putting his hand on Daphne's shoulder, he said with a big sigh, "Okay." They left home. Facing the community center, Steve looked lovingly at the greenhouses he had helped design. Clara's home was the second building around the corner. They arrived there in no time, and entered without knocking.

"Welcome, Steve. I am glad you could come," said Clara with a big warm smile. "We are ready to start, so make yourself comfortable on a BackJack, a mattress, or a chair. Stanly will be happy to have more masculine energy in the room."

"I really don't have much time. I need to go back to my work," he answered, looking around to see who else was in attendance.

"I understand, Steve. We all appreciate your devotion to your vocation and your patients. But based on my experience, when you are trying to solve a difficult problem, it is beneficial to get away from the usual way you approach it and try to tackle it from a different angle. You never know where the solution will come from. However, I understand your concern. I will start with a short explanation, and we will get quickly to the journey."

As he sat by Daphne, Steve noticed Liz and Vanessa smiling at him, both of them wrapped in a blanket and waiting.

For Steve's sake, Clara summarized what the regular participants had heard many times. She described shamanism as the oldest spiritual tradition shared by our ancestors on every continent who believed in animism, meaning that everything has a spirit and you can be in touch with these spirits to ask for help and advice. "The tribe's shaman," she said, "would undergo a long, arduous training process by an experienced shaman to help his or her tribe as a healer, counselor, and yes, even prophet. About eighty years ago, our country opened to non-monotheistic traditions like Buddhism. People acknowledged both the value of these practices to the seeking individuals and the need to translate them to their contemporaries. They did not consider themselves as shamans, much less their students, but as shamanism practitioners."

Steve, who had not known what to expect, as Daphne had never told him about her experience, was surprised. *What have I gotten myself into?* He respected Clara and Stanley enough not to show any misgiving. He listened patiently as Clara continued.

"So, think about the shamanic journey as a form of meditation, where the sound of percussion—a drum or a rattle—helps you to enter a mild trance state. Today, Stanly will drum for us, and I will journey with you. Start by setting an intent for the journey. It can be a question you want an answer to or an issue you wish to resolve. Be as specific as you can. The most important thing is to get yourselves out of the way and let things happen. Don't worry about making things up. Everything that occurs in your journey happens for a reason. You can travel to the lower world through any opening, like a cave, a body of water, or a tree trunk. There, you will meet your animal spirit guides. You can travel to the middle world, which is where we are but in an alternate reality, or the world of dreams. You can also journey to the upper world, where you will meet one or more teachers. A teacher can be a religious figure who is meaningful to you, a famous healer, an ancestor, or your higher self, whoever can help with the issue you set as your intent. The journey will last fifteen to twenty minutes. When the drumming rhythm changes, this is the callback. It's time to thank your teachers and guides and then come back to the room. I suggest that beginners start journeying to the lower world and get to know their animal spirit guides. Remember, there is no right or wrong way to do it. Everybody's experience is different. Some see images, others tend to hear messages, and some just have a sense of knowing and understanding. Be open to receiving anything that happens. Don't try to impose things, but you can ask questions. Let's start. We will discuss our experiences later."

As Clara was talking, it occurred to Steve that, not unlike Clara, he pursued knowledge of alternative methods of healing, his area being herbs and plants used across the globe to cure ailments. He thought that maybe there were different kinds of knowledge that our culture began to ignore when the scientific way of thinking entered into the equation, those other methods being pushed aside as superstitions. So, he decided to follow Clara's instructions and give shamanic journeying his best shot.

Clara closed the shutters and darkened the room. Stanly started drumming. Steve closed his eyes and imagined a cave, which he used to go down as instructed. His intent was to understand and find a cure for the strange disease that had just presented at the hospital. He did see a nice peaceful place down there, filled with trees and plenty of flowers and herbs, which to his surprise he could even smell. However, no animal had shown up and he'd received no answer. His thoughts drifted to the hospital and his garden, and he reminded himself repeatedly to go back to the journey. At some point, he told himself that, unsurprisingly, journeying did not work for him. He decided to relax, rest, and wait for the callback, hoping that it would happen soon. All of a sudden, he saw a beautiful white mushroom appearing in front of him.

"Who are you?"

"You know me; I will help you. I am waiting for you in your garden."

A sharp realization penetrated him. "Of course. Oh my God!" He stood up and ran out of the door, before the callback.

However, he could not have missed Stanly's exclamation—"Eureka!"

Steve ran home to the experimental part of his garden and saw the mushroom. He picked a few mushrooms and knew he had to cook them and add some other herbs and some marijuana for relaxation. When the soupy remedy was ready, he placed it in a tightly closed container and rushed to the hospital. He ran to the third floor, swiftly passed the astonished nurses, put on his hazmat suit, and approached the patients. He spoke to them softly, had them smell the medicine, and then fed them two spoonfuls each.

"I hope it helps," he told the nurse who looked confused about what was happening. The three fell asleep about fifteen minutes later. When they woke up several hours later, they felt better and started eating and talking.

Steve wrote down the instructions for preparing the remedy, including suggestions to use powder or tincture if they could not find fresh mushrooms and herbs, and promptly sent these to all the health institutions. All the hospitals that tried it reported recovery. Family members who came to visit their loved ones did not know how to thank him. He just smiled and said, "I am glad I could help." The neighbors told him that he was Oasis's hero, and Daphne said she was proud to be his partner.

The media started interviewing him, and his reputation grew across Colorado. The public had been awaiting a hero, and the journalists were willing to provide one, but Steve, the reluctant hero, did not share their enthusiasm. "It's too early to celebrate. I am glad I was capable of assisting with this outbreak, but until we find out what caused it, we are in danger of more outbreaks that may or may not respond to the treatment. There is much more work to do."

CHAPTER 8

THE SURPRISE

James Callahan, a.k.a Gene Kerrigan, started getting used to the life in California but could not fathom that he would be able to stay there for too long. He made sure his antennae were ready to receive any news from any source. Having learned his lesson the hard way, he firmly believed that knowing what was going on was a matter of life and death.

There was no doubt in his mind that the Chinese success was due to the inability of the government in Washington, DC, to cope with the multiple disasters, coupled with the failure of the local government to deal with them. He'd heard numerous stories about people who had lost everything, who had been helped by the Chinese, and who were now living a modest life in residences that were as disaster-proof as possible. No matter how much he inquired, he heard no stories of extreme exploitation or cruelty. It seems that the Chinese had been handling their increasing control of the population better than the OD had. All they wanted was the free immigration of Chinese people into the state, and they got it. The Chinese government wisely built Chinese-only communities that were as self-sufficient as possible so that the Californians would be led to believe that they were being helped but paying nothing in return.

Callahan's gut feeling, however, sent him a different message: *All these good feelings and apparent harmony is illusory and one day will blow up. Californians will eventually start sensing that they are becoming a minority in their own country, and what will happen then? And what if China believes it has enough support and decides to annex the western portion of the United States or send an army? Will people still feel thankful for the help?* He did not think so. *By then, it would be much harder to do anything about it. And resistance would probably be punished as harshly as it is on the mainland.* He felt almost like a traitor helping the Chinese in their endeavor. To his chagrin, he had not been given any chance during his half-year stay to provide any support to the existing population.

Ecological Builders management appreciated Callahan's expertise and his apparent effort to teach sustainable building to anybody who was willing to listen. He was friendly enough to engage in small talk and tell amusing stories that he chose carefully, making sure that they neither revealed his opinions nor irritated those in power.

Half a year into his tenure, the projects on the site were completed, and the company started development about one hundred miles north. They finally provided Callahan with a car, as this was the most efficient way to send him north and still have him around when needed. They had warned him, however, not even to dream about escaping. Their technology had his fingerprints, and they would find him anywhere if he tried to escape. Callahan decided to enjoy his greater freedom and not to raise suspicion.

The avid developer relished starting a new project and guiding the first stages of the design. Part of his preparation included traveling around the site and studying the neighboring communities, since he believed that every new community should be integrated with the existing ones. He was aware, of course, that for the time being, the Chinese residents were remaining pretty well out of sight, but he believed that eventually they would have to interact with their neighbors.

On one of his excursions, in a small local store, he noticed an invitation to participate in a Native American ceremony, which would take place later in the evening. Although he was not particularly interested in indigenous cultures or spirituality, he was curious enough to find out how the Miwok had coped with the disasters that he paid the entry fee, described as a donation to the tribe. He arrived early and examined the simple but functional homes and the adjacent cultivated areas of fruits, vegetables, and corn. Unlike with his designs, he noticed that the tribe had hardly any greenhouses. This he attributed to the fact that they suffered relatively less from natural disaster. His impression was that the people were healthy and content. He entered the arena looking forward to the performance.

The haunting sound of a flute filled the air, and the audience turned still at once. It was a unique mix of traditional and contemporary music composed by the tribe's most talented musician. *It's so beautiful. It helps you forget about the ugliness of the world outside,* Callahan thought, relaxing in his seat on the wooden bench. He looked at the audience of mostly Native American, but quite a few white people; all of them seemed more serene.

The tribe's shaman stood up slowly, and a choir dressed in traditional Native clothes appeared on the other side of the arena.

The shaman lamented: "O Mother Earth, we, the people of earth, have polluted all the treasures that you have bestowed on us. We filled the air with smoke and poisonous gases. We contaminated the pure water of your springs. We defiled the vast oceans with streams of foul material. We intruded into your bosom and excavated your treasures, while giving you back all the toxins we wanted to dispose of. We failed to guard the sacred soil our life depends on and covered it with deadly chemicals and crops you never intended."

The chorus responded: "Please forgive us and have pity on us."

The shaman continued: "We are sick. Many of us died prematurely, and evil powers govern us. We are too weak to defend ourselves and powerless to protect you. All we can do is pray and ask for your mercy."

The chorus responded: "Please forgive us for the sake of our children."

The exchange continued, and the melancholic flute melody penetrated every cell in Callahan's body. With eyes full of tears, he breathed heavily. *What is happening to me? Am I becoming sentimental as I grow older?* His habitual cynicism that had always shielded him from any extreme emotional response could not overcome his emotional upheaval. He felt dizzy, yet deeply connected with his innermost essence. Although he did not need any lecture about humankind's influence on climate change and the ensuing catastrophes, he had never felt so touched and real.

The ceremony continued with traditional powwow dances, accompanied by traditional songs and lyrics. Then the magic disappeared. Callahan did not know what the powwow ceremony meant for the tribe. What he sensed was a powerful declaration of tribal identity: "This is who we are, and that's how it is going to stay."

I wish I could feel that way, he reflected, feeling disconnected from any human group he could have called his tribe.

A few days later he was back in Merced and was called to Delun Wei's office.

"I heard that you enjoy cultural events," Delun said sarcastically. "Here is a ticket for a higher-quality performance."

"Thanks," responded Callahan, realizing that this was Delun Wei's way of telling him that he was being followed and that he had better not try anything foolish. The ticket was an invitation to the show of a Chinese dancing group that recently arrived from China's mainland.

"See you tomorrow at the show," Wei added, observing Callahan's response.

Maintaining his poker face, Callahan responded, "Sure. See you tomorrow."

The following evening, Callahan put on his best suit, which was pretty worn given what it and its owner had experienced together; combed his unkempt salt-and-pepper hair and beard, which had grown somewhat wild; and then went outside and reluctantly started his car. He did not care much about the show and dreaded another encounter with Sophie. *I hope Sophie convinced Delun that I am just an old boyfriend,* he thought on his way to the event. But he knew better. The Chinese had collected a lot of information about him and probably about his family as well before they put their hands on him. Delun must have had at least some suspicions.

The hall was full of people dressed elegantly, most of them Chinese, but also others who had been invited by their Chinese employers. Callahan looked for his seat at the back of the orchestra section. After finding it, he started looking around for his boss and Sophie. He did not have to wait for a long time. As he glanced to his left, he saw both of them passing by his seat. He nodded to Delun

Wei, who seemed to be looking for him, as he knew his seat number. Delun returned the nod very formally. Sophie, in a gorgeous dress that fit her very well, was looking forward. Her attempt to hide her emotions revealed her stress and fear.

The orchestra started playing Chinese music, the curtain was opened, and the performers with beautifully designed outfits performed their art. Callahan had seen Chinese American group performances before when he lived in East and wondered if this was going to be any different. He needed to be able to have something to say about it if he happened to meet Delun during the intermission. The performance was very modern in content, depicting a great and benevolent China. Unsurprisingly, it included a dance showing how the Chinese are helping the Californians. *Pure propaganda,* he thought, wondering what was going to happen next.

Finally, the lights went up, and he went out to buy a drink. He knew he should not appear suspicious, so he looked around to find acquaintances. Bob from his team was standing alone sipping a drink. Callahan hurried to greet him. From the corner of his eye, he saw Delun approaching the vendors by himself. Chatting with Bob, Callahan also noticed that Delun purchased only one drink. He knew this meant trouble.

"Did you receive the ticket from Delun for good behavior as well?" asked Bob, his back to Delun.

"Pretty much. And he is walking toward us."

Bob turned around, greeted Delun, and extolled the performance. Delun seemed to be aware that it was sheer flattery, but then this was what he had expected.

"And what do you think, Kerrigan? Isn't it better than the hoo-ha you attended a few days ago?"

"Thanks again for the ticket. I very much enjoyed the costumes and skilled performance," he answered, ignoring the insulting comparison.

"Where is your lovely wife?" asked Bob.

Callahan felt butterflies in his gut but stayed calm.

"I asked her not to join me during intermission." He was emotionless and stern. "Enjoy the rest of the show," he added. Then he turned away and disappeared into the crowd.

"Wrong question," said James.

The bell calling to audience to go back inside was a savior.

"What is wrong, Kerrigan?"

"I wish I knew."

+ ◆ ◆ ◆ ◆ ◆ +

Callahan was glad to see his son, who had come for a surprise visit during a school vacation. Jacob, or Jerome as he was called now, studied architecture and community design, had a girlfriend named Marina, and seemed quite happy. He told his father that Sophie was mad at him for helping the OD and cheating on her. Jacob had not heard her speak a kind word about his father since they'd left. Luckily, he was old enough to remember a loving and devoted father and could not wait to meet him. Callahan was glad to hear that Delun Wei was treating his mother and him well and had paid for his college studies.

When Callahan asked what they had been through since they'd left East and before Sophie married Delun Wei, Jacob became visibly upset.

"It was terrible. We were attacked by a gang that took all our money and belongings and raped Mom. We were lucky to survive. We both worked for food and shelter and moved on when there was no work to do. We were cold and hungry all the time. Eventually, Mom befriended a tracker who took her to California on a business trip. She found a job as a waitress in a restaurant frequented by many Chinese officers. That's where she met Delun Wei. He told her that he had lost his wife and children to a terrible earthquake in China. She relayed to him that you had died and she had escaped from the OD. When he proposed, she agreed, and they got married."

"I am sorry you had to go through this, Jacob. It's certainly not your fault. And after I told Delun at the party that I and Sophie, or Sonya, knew each other, did he ask further questions? What if he finds out that you have visited me?"

"I know that he is suspicious and has started mistrusting her. She did not tell me the details. I was not there when she told him that you had died. But when he mentioned it later, I did not deny it,

86

because I did not want to get her into trouble. She has suffered a lot, and Delun is her chance for a comfortable and safe life."

"Does she love him?"

"I don't know. She needs him. She puts in a lot of acting into the relationship."

"Does he think she loves him?"

"He sure did before you showed up. He would not have paid for my college if he had not. And I genuinely like him. He is a good man. I didn't think I'd ever see you again. Now their relationship is tense. I'm not sure exactly what's going on. I try to stay out of it."

After seeing his son, Callahan felt the urgent need to find a better place to live, not just for himself but also for Jacob. The news he heard every day just confirmed his suspicions about trouble on the horizon.

<hr />

Delun Wei was an excellent judge of character. He had always known whom he could trust and how to address different kinds of people. That was what kept him alive and capable of overriding the disasters, although his family had not been as lucky. They were killed in a flood when he was away on a business trip, and since then, he has suffered the guilt and shame of not having been there to protect them. He did trust Sonya, maybe because he was smitten by her beauty and vulnerability. But since the party, and the look on her and Kerrigan's faces when they saw each other, he had ceased trusting her. Disbelieving her story about Callahan being an old boyfriend, Delun used his connections to investigate her past. It took about a month, during which time his loving treatment of her turned into an angry silence.

Then he received the report that confirmed his suspicions. He found out that Sonya was Sophie Callahan, the wife of Gene Kerrigan. She had lied to him when she told him that her former husband had died. Additionally, the report mentioned that she had escaped with her son and without her husband to Central. It was not hard for Delun to figure out why she had tried to conceal this part of her life. The description of her miserable life in Central was compatible with what she had told him, but it was the result of her doing. He decided to talk with Kerrigan, previously Callahan, before facing his wife.

Delun Wei asked Callahan to come to his office and report about his work.

"I found out that Sonya is your lost wife, Sophie," he said, as soon as Callahan, who had arrived swiftly carrying some reports, closed the office door behind him.

"She was my wife. She left me and took my son with her. Quite frankly, I did not believe I would see her or my son again, or that we would get back together even if I did find her. I assumed that she was hiding somewhere in Central and had probably met somebody. The last place I expected to meet her was your home. She was kind enough to send me a copy of the divorce she obtained as soon as she reached Central. Not that it helps. The document describes a divorce between James and Sophia Callahan, but both of us have different names now. Anyway, she is not my wife. She is my ex-wife."

The report did not mention the divorce, so Delun had just found out that he had married a divorcée, not a widow, which was better than being married to another man's wife.

"Since you admit that her son is your son, I think that it's just fair to ask you to pay for his college expenses. I took pity on the poor orphan and had started treating him like a son, just to find out that I'd been fooled."

"Nobody fooled you, sir. Sophie did not believe that she or Jacob would ever see me again. She just tried to create a more acceptable life story. I know that Jacob appreciates everything you have done for him and his mom. He is very fond of you as well. I am sincerely thankful for what you have done for him, but since I've now found him, I agree that it is my job, not yours, to support him. I will do my best with the salary I receive from you. Just a reminder: it was not my decision to come here and interfere with your life. I was kidnapped and was told to work with you or else."

"I am glad that we have reached an understanding about Jerome, whom you call Jacob. I will see if the authorities will approve of moving you north, closer to where you currently work. Don't expect a raise anytime soon. And if you try to escape, Jacob will suffer the consequences. That's all; you are free to go."

———————— ✦✦✦✦✦✦ ————————

Sonya returned home from a visit with the doctor in a state of shock. She'd felt sick, hoping that it was nothing serious, but nothing had prepared her for the diagnosis. She was pregnant with Delun's child at age forty-two. The doctor told her to take better care of her health and avoid stress, but how could she? She started preparing Delun's favorite dish for dinner; set the table with a lovely tablecloth, flowers, candles, and a bottle of wine; wore her flattering dress; and just prayed. Knowing that he was suspicious and was probably investigating her past, she contemplated telling him the truth after he'd heard the good news. Luckily, the test showed that the conception occurred six weeks ago, that is, two weeks before the fateful party.

"What's the occasion? What are we celebrating?" he asked sarcastically when he entered the house.

"I will let you know as soon as you sit at the table," she answered, trying hard to smile and look cheerful.

"I am in no mood to celebrate anything. I have just spoken to your ex. He admitted it. You lied to me, Sonya! I trusted you and did my best for you and Jerome, just to find out that it is all a big fat lie."

Sonya started shaking. She became pale and sat at the table. "I am pregnant with your child. I am supposed to avoid stress or I will lose the baby. I love you. ... I love you, Delun. I was afraid that if you found out that I left my husband, you would never even come close to me. Besides the fact that I loathed the work that he did for the OD and what the OD did to the people, I knew that he cheated on me in every city he stayed in, including visiting nasty sex clubs. Our relationship was bad, and we fought constantly. I took advantage of a daylong trip that he had taken for a work meeting and left East. During my stay in Central, I was even more miserable and questioned the wisdom of my decision to leave him. The only time I've been happy is when I am with you." She sobbed quietly.

"Which doctor did you see?"

"Your friend Dr. Chen."

"He is not a gynecologist!"

"Of course not! He is our family doctor. Not in my wildest dreams did I think that I was pregnant, although my period was late. My ex and I tried for years to conceive another child and were unsuccessful. Who thought that I could get pregnant at forty-two?"

––––––––– ‣‣♦♦♦♦‣‣ –––––––––

The telephone rang.

"Hello, Delun. This is Dr. Chen. Have you heard the news?"

Delun uttered an unenthusiastic yes.

"I did not want to scare your wife, but I am not sure she will be able to complete the pregnancy. Her general health is poor, mainly because of malnutrition. She seems to be under stress and probably does not eat well. She has lost a lot of weight since her last visit. I prescribed some supplements, but that's all I can do. I suggest that she see Dr. Lu. She is a good gynecologist and a kind and friendly woman."

"How long has she been pregnant?"

"Six to seven weeks."

It was quiet on both sides of the line. Finally, Dr. Chen said, "If you do not have any more questions, good night. Call me if you need any help."

Delun had noticed that Sonya retreated to the bedroom when he was talking to the doctor. He tried to remember what had happened two to three weeks before the party. It seemed to be so long ago. Then he remembered. He reminisced about a romantic full-moon night when he took Sonya to a beautiful rose garden and then to an expensive restaurant. She was glowing and wore a beautiful dress, the same one she was wearing tonight. They made love passionately that night.

It must be my child! How come I am not happy and not even touched by her misery?

He entered the bedroom. Sonya was asleep, breathing heavily and unevenly. Returning to the dining room, he examined the beautiful table and helped himself to a hefty serving of the tasty food. Delun was well aware that she had tried hard to create a romantic evening and that he had spoiled it. Sitting in his favorite rocking chair and watching the news broadcast, he had to admit that she had a point. Had he known that she had run away from her husband, he would have never approached her. It was her vulnerability, which reminded him of how his late wife must have felt when she was left alone with the kids when disaster struck, that attracted him to Sonya and made him want to protect her. Now, he could no longer feel like her savior, only as the man whom she'd fooled. Of course, she needed help, but it was because of her decision to leave her husband, not because of a disaster.

Then he contemplated the possibility of losing the baby. He knew that she was under stress and had lost weight. Did he want to start a family with her after what he knew about her now? Sonya was screaming in her sleep. He was aware that if he wanted the baby, he had to change his attitude fast. Delun returned to the bedroom and looked at Sonya's agonized face. He caressed her hair and lay down beside her.

When she woke up in the morning, Delun was on his way to work. She found a note: "Thanks for the tasty dinner. Take good care of yourself. See you tonight." She noticed that he had put the tablecloth in the laundry and removed the candles, wine, and flowers from the table as if last night had never happened. She moved slowly, determined to follow the doctor's order to relax and eat well. She had to force herself to eat the healthy food she prepared, and even then she could finish only half of the plate. She knew that if she lost the baby, the marriage would be over and she would have nowhere to go.

The phone rang.

"Hi, Mom. I have just talked to Dad. He told me that Delun asked him if you were married and he confirmed, assuming that Delun already knew anyway. Delun will stop paying my college tuition, and Dad will do his best to help. He does not make much nowadays and does not expect a raise anytime soon, so I don't know how much he will be able to support me. However, I feel relieved that the truth is out and I can see my father without being afraid of raising Delun's suspicion."

"He talked with me too, and it was not pretty. I wish I had not had to tell him the news that I am pregnant, but I wanted to let him know before Dr. Chen contacted him."

"You are what?!"

"I know it sounds strange for you to have a half-brother or -sister at age twenty. It sounds bizarre to me too and, even more than that, scary. The doctor seemed to be concerned about my nervousness and poor health. I am trying to relax. If I don't, I will lose the baby."

"Did you want to become pregnant?"

"I did not think I could. For years your father and I tried to conceive another child. It took Delun less than six months. I have not used any precautions for years. Only now is a terrible time. We are not as happy as we used to be, and I am not sure I will get the support I need to carry the child to term. I feel sick and weak."

"Can I come to see you now? I think that Delun would be unhappy to see me, so I will try to visit when I have no classes and he is out."

"Sure, you can come. And please buy me the supplement the doctor prescribed. I will spell it for you. It is something Chinese."

Sonya enjoyed Jerome's visit. She became somewhat more relaxed as they talked about school and his new girlfriend. However, one thing made her deathly worried. He told her that when he spoke with his father, Callahan had mentioned that he was being followed, probably by the OD. When James visited a bar, he heard two men asking the barman about his whereabouts. The Chinese were following him too, but they didn't need to ask the barman. Sonya knew that the OD killed fugitives from the East to discourage people from running away. She and her son were fugitives as well, and if what Jerome was telling her was true, all three of them were in danger. She wondered how she could discuss it with Delun without making him angry just by mentioning her ex.

She decided to get a new dress in a store she liked but had not visited for a few months because it was a somewhat long drive. When she arrived at the area, the closest parking lot she found was quite far from the store, but the weather was pleasant, so she thought it would be good exercise to walk to the store. As she started walking, she noticed that the place looked more run down than the last time she had been there. About halfway through, she encountered three young men approaching her, calling her names, whistling, and laughing. Contemplating what would be her best bet, either going into the store or back to her car, she noticed a policeman about two hundred feet ahead and rushed toward him. She explained the situation and asked him to accompany her to the store.

"This is their neighborhood. I cannot tell them what to do. I cannot leave my post either. You should not have come here."

She called Delun and frantically explained what had happened.

"I am on my way. Don't leave the policeman."

"My husband is on his way. Please make sure that they do not hurt me."

The three approached and continued insulting Sonya. They also groped her. The cop begged them to stop, but they just laughed at him. It seemed that he was their buddy from the neighborhood and they were not going to take orders from him. The terrified Sonya was relieved to see Delun's car approaching. She hoped that the ordeal would end soon. Delun stopped with his brakes shrieking and jumped out of the car.

"What is going on?" he asked the cop. "Why aren't you performing your duty and arresting these thugs?" Turning to his wife, he said, "Sonya, get in the car!"

"Sonya, get in the car," the three men said, mimicking him. "Couldn't you find a better man than this yellow, whore?"

Sonya was terrified to see that just as Delun started walking toward the driver's seat, one of the youngsters pulled a knife. Delun pulled a handgun from his pocket and shot. She could see that he hit one the thugs, who fell to the ground. Delun got back in the car and drove away without looking back.

"I will ask our people to retrieve your car. What on earth brought you here?"

"I wanted to buy a new dress in the store across the street. That was where I bought the one you like so much. I had no idea that the place has deteriorated so much. What is going to happen about the shooting?"

"Don't worry; our people will take care of it."

"I am worried for more than one reason. First, Jerome told me that my ex believes that some OD spies are following him. If they can locate him, they can locate Jerome and me. We are fugitives as well."

"I know. He told his team manager, who informed me. We arrested two people and will make sure that no suspicious people come near you or him."

"Thanks, Delun. You know, when I lived in Central, people could not trust each other. Anybody might have been a spy. I did not think I would have to worry about that here."

"I can't believe that people would be so ungrateful after everything we have done to help them to cope with the disasters."

"That is the other thing I am worried about, Delun. The more people you bring in, the more you make people feel like minorities in their own country. They feel conquered without war. You cannot avoid the growing hostility even when the newcomers live in enclaves away from mainstream America. Their sheer numbers make them conspicuous."

"What side are you on?" he asked.

"I am married to a Chinese man and my child will be half Chinese. I want everybody to live in peace and harmony."

CHAPTER 9

ATWELL

Felix Atwell, the appointed president of the United States, sat on his carefully selected chair in the Oval Office feeling pleased with himself. He had succeeded at creating a good relationship with Ernest Sullivan, the new director of intelligence and surveillance, and Louis Folk, director of law and order. Although he was quite aware that the common fear of "being taken care of" had a lot to do with this bond, he believed that a true friendship had grown out of it. Three months after the meeting in the Hub, the East was unrecognizable. Against all the odds, and with a meager budget, they had established OD control over the southeastern states and had improved intelligence and surveillance.

Being aware of people's misery under the OD regime, Atwell thought about ways to ease it. More than his benevolence, it was Atwell's pragmatism that led him to believe that improving people's lives was his best guarantee for preventing unrest and maintaining order. Among other initiatives, he instructed the director of health and wellness to start planning a minimal health-care program to help those who could not afford medical care.

He also met with delegates from Harvard and MIT and promised them that he would do his best under the circumstances. He encouraged them to develop some operable low-budget options for improving people's lives. He was most impressed by a guy named David who represented a Cambridge group of MIT graduates calling itself the Geek Clique, which seemed to have already made some plans that could be executed.

Still, something was not right. He had not received an invitation to the Hub and had not even heard from Oliphant, the OD chairman, for three months. That was quite unusual. He tried to suppress any premonition of danger, convincing himself that doing a great job would guarantee approval and appreciation from the OD. Since he was not supposed to initiate contact with Oliphant unless it was an emergency, and knowing the guy's adherence to protocol, he reluctantly obliged and did not discuss his plans with him. *Is Oliphant displeased with my plans?* he wondered.

Atwell also knew that the people close to him were loyal to the OD, not necessarily because they disliked him, but because they feared retribution in the event they failed to report everything that happened around them. So, Atwell gave up his past arrogant behavior and started treating everybody around him with kindness and respect. However, Atwell was not sure that there was even one person in the administration he could trust. Therefore, he disclosed as little as possible and acted as a very loyal servant of the OD.

He did discuss his concerns with Sarah, his wife, who asked him for her sake and the sake of their children to resign from his job, saying that there was no way to do his job right and prevail. She was terrified by the stories about people who disappeared or were "taken care of." Atwell's attempts to persuade her that such a thing would not happen to him made her even more fearful. He knew that she was not convinced, as he saw the fearful look on her face and heard her say over again that he needed to quit before it was too late. He did not believe that all was well and knew that she was smart enough to figure out that he was just trying to calm her down. So, they created an escape plan, just in case, including an emergency signal. Three consecutive blank messages from him would mean that she needs to fetch the kids and execute the plan.

Suddenly, dark thoughts disturbed his good mood. *Something is wrong today. People in the office are speaking more softly not looking each other in the eye. No jokes or laughter. Employees seem to distance themselves from me. I am sure I am not making this up. What do they know that I don't?*

As he was mulling over his options, he saw an urgent message from Governor Adam Hickman of Colorado. "A missile from your area hit close to Denver. Luckily it caused no harm. We do not want a war, but if you want it, you will get it. Don't dare to invade our territory. We are not going to be your OD's puppets."

He sank into his chair, his heart beating wildly. Having no control of the discharge of missiles, he knew nothing about it. *I should be cautious,* he thought.

Then, a news message flashed on his screen. "A Russian missile hit Colorado. We should brace for war, because Central is blaming us for the attack."

Atwell was sure that whoever had sent this message had done so in coordination with the OD. Of course, like everybody else, he knew that nobody would believe this announcement, because the Russians had been too busy in Europe and had no intention of opening a new front in the United States. But obviously he did not intend to doubt it publicly.

He sent three blank messages to Sarah.

The cabinet meeting would start within thirty minutes. Atwell's confidence that he was in control gave way to vague anxiety. "Mr. Oliphant is on the line," Norma's voice said over the intercom. Atwell thought he sensed her anxiety.

He picked up the phone. "Good morning, Mister Oliphant. I am glad you called. I have been wanting to discuss with you the missile attack on Central and some of my plans ..."

"Cut it, Atwell! I know all about your plans. You should follow instructions, not develop initiatives to help people! You did an excellent job expanding our control all over the East. Now, I expect you to do as well extending it to the West."

"Oliphant, I guess you saw Hickman's message. What should I answer?"

"Tell them that the missile was delivered from Russia. We observed the trajectory and can provide a map to prove it. I have just sent it to you on the secret info line. They are not going to believe it, of course. In your upcoming cabinet meeting, you should discuss the expansion plan. Don't you dare spend time and money on welfare plans! Is that understood?"

"Yes, sir! I have no military experience, and your endeavor calls for an expert. I think I should resign and let you appoint somebody more qualified for the job."

"Don't dare to think about resignation. When we need to replace you, we will take care of things." Atwell felt cold and immobile, as if he had just spoken to the angel of death. He fetched the missile trajectory map sent by Oliphant and dictated a short message to Governor Hickman.

"The missile was sent by the Russians, as evidenced by the attached trajectory map captured by our technicians. Please don't jump to conclusions. We do not want a war either."

Atwell was walking toward his office door, sending a yearning look to the cloudless blue sky and the wise old oak tree, with which he suddenly wished to trade places. The picture of Sarah and the kids crossed his mind when he felt as if electrical waves were traversing his body and he fell on the floor.

Half an hour later, the OD broadcasting system announced that the president had died from a sudden stroke.

* * * * * * *

Sarah looked at the phone. She had hoped that this moment would never arrive, but here it was, three blank messages from Felix. She called Henry, their family friend and confidant and her secret admirer, using the same code, to which he answered: "On my way." Then she sent the signal to her high school and middle school sons. They knew that they would have to leave class as if going to the bathroom and then go look for Henry. Making sure that all the shutters were tightly closed and locked, Sarah started frantically packing clothes, food, kitchenware, and bedding—whatever she could fit into their family motor home. She fetched all the cash, family pictures, and formal documents she could find.

Although Atwell was the appointed president, the OD had not allowed the family to live in the White House. The president went to work exactly like everybody else. That suited Sarah very well. She did not crave the first lady role and knew that the more anonymous they were, the safer they would be.

Henry and the children arrived from a secret entrance two miles away from their residence. The secret entrance led to an underground road beneath their formal garage, into the secret garage where they kept their escape vehicle. By the time they entered, Sarah's home screen had broadcasted the news about the president's death. She was in total shock. Sure that Felix would somehow join them before they left, she had packed his best clothes. She did not believe for a minute that it was a natural death. She was convinced that he'd been murdered before he'd had time to escape.

Henry said softly, "Hurry. We have no time to waste. Pack the last things and rush to the car."

The children gave their rooms a last, gloomy look. Paul, the elder, picked up his guitar, Danny picked up his running trophies, and they headed to the motor home. Henry sat in the driver's seat, and Sarah sat frozen beside him. The children were crying silently in the back.

"They are probably already waiting for us outside," said Henry as he rolled the car onto the underground road. They exited from a different outlet than the one they had entered, and just before they emerged into the daylight, Henry activated the stealth feature. The car moved unseen. Henry selected remote country roads with a low volume of traffic to avoid a collision.

The heavy silence was broken by Henry, who informed Sarah and the children that he was going to activate the camouflage device to turn the shiny white vehicle into an old brownish one with an Illinois license plate. "We must use the highway if we want to be on the other side by tonight. They are probably looking for us already, so I have to drive as fast as I possibly can."

The children started asking questions, and Sarah explained that their father had been killed by evil people who loathed his plans to help people. She repeated many times the story of a loving father who had thought ahead of time to create an escape plan, as his family's safety, not his own, was his primary concern. Sarah wanted to make sure that the youngsters remembered their father as a hero. As she was talking, she put together some lunch for everybody and gave the kids their favorite snacks.

As they approached the East–Central border, it started raining. Visibility deteriorated. Henry noticed some commotion near the border and decided to circumvent this passage. Luckily, he knew the area well. He exited the highway and, with one touch, changed the vehicle's look again, this time into a sporty maroon motor home. Half an hour later they crossed an old, less used bridge over the Mississippi in stealth mode.

"We are in Central!" declared Henry proudly. Everyone gave a sigh of relief. "However, we are not safe and will have to hide. I will try to reach a friend who lives nearby." Since they had left all their communication devices at home, to avoid being detected, Henry purchased a Central mobile phone and called his friend. He had to wait two hours until he could park the motor home in the large garage, two hours away from the nightmare and two hours closer to their freedom.

A simple dinner awaited them, and of course the news. The OD-authorized broadcasting system, the only one legal in East, announced President Atwell's tragic, untimely death. The announcements were accompanied by solemn music.

Sarah could barely eat while listening to the news, but she encouraged the children to eat. In the depths of her devastation and grief was a strong determination to make sure that their children would grow up safe in a free society and remember their father as a loving man who had tried to do his best to fight evil. She was thankful that Henry had gotten them skillfully to Central when the anchor blamed Central for kidnapping Atwell's widow and children and promised the listeners that the government would do everything possible to locate them and return them to Washington, DC. Then she heard the details of the funeral. The next day, the coffin would be placed in the northern entrance to the White House, and people would be able to pass by Atwell's coffin and pay their final respects for two days. On the third day, the coffin would be driven to Arlington National Cemetery, the place of Atwell's final rest. Sarah made sure that she would have the equipment to watch the news while they were driving inland.

The following day, Henry and Sarah were told that Governor Hickman wanted to see them and was offering them shelter. They thanked their hosts and then were on their way to Colorado. It was a rainy, dreary day. Sarah felt as if the sky was participating in their grief. They turned on the news. The camera was trained on long lines of people waiting patiently for their turn to pass by the coffin, all somber and many sobbing. Sarah hugged the children, relieved that they were able to see how much people loved their father. After about half an hour, the broadcasting returned to the usual programming.

Early that afternoon, just as they entered Denver, they heard that the OD had decided to limit public access to the funeral for "safety reasons." Only dignitaries would be allowed to pass by the coffin the following day.

They drove straight to the governor's mansion. The governor greeted them cordially, expressed his sincere condolences to the family, and then asked a lot of questions about East, especially what they knew about the missile attack.

"Your husband—sorry, late husband—sent us a message accompanied by a map indicating that the missile was sent from Russia. Of course, it does not make sense. What do you think happened?"

"I have not heard about the missile attack. You have to understand that Felix had no control of missiles. They were all under the OD's control. He probably heard about it yesterday before his assassination. I hope you do not believe the stroke story any more than you believe the Russian missile one. Felix told you what they had ordered him to say. He was trying to save his life and ours. The last time I spoke with him was before he left in the morning. We both had been concerned about our safety for a long time. The OD 'took care of' anybody who showed incompetence or disobedience. I warned Felix that his programs to help people would anger the OD. They are ruthless and want to rule over a mass of submissive slaves. He was not a hero, but a pragmatist who believed that unnecessary cruelty is stupid and that happier people would be easier, not harder, to control. Hmm, I almost forgot. A week ago he gave me a map to be used by the right people. I believe you would be the best protector of the map."

She opened a hidden compartment in a big bag and retrieved a carefully folded map covered with plastic. "The OD underground headquarters!"

Hickman glanced at the map, thinking that it could not have arrived at a better time.

"How did you get it? Are you sure it is valid and accurate?"

"Felix gave it to me just in case, because he did not trust the OD.

This is the map he used to visit the place. His last visit was about three months ago. You see, they eventually exterminated everybody who was involved with them, before he even suspected it. Felix suspected he would be next, because that's what happened to others in similar positions."

"Thanks, Sarah. We will put your gift to good use. I believe that Felix was assassinated, as do most people in East. I have just received the information that rumors about your husband's efforts to improve people's lives, for which he was assassinated, spread like wildfire in East and turned him into an overnight hero, a martyr, and a symbol of resistance to the OD. That explains the unexpected number of people who traveled to Washington to thank him, and the OD's decision to cancel the second day's visitation to prevent social upheaval.

"Now your safety is the utmost priority. We have an underground shelter for refugees wanted by the OD. For your safety, please stay there. It is very comfortable, equipped with schools, an elaborate communications center, a gym, and restaurants—just about everything you may need. If you need something you cannot get there, please let us know, and we will do our best to provide it. You may meet people whom you know. As far as the OD are concerned, we have never seen you and have no clue of your whereabouts."

The governor's secretary led them to their underground apartment. On the way, Sarah noticed a familiar figure. "It cannot be!" The man approached them. "President Rockwell!" exclaimed Sarah, stunned. "You are alive!"

"I am, and I am deeply sorry about your husband's death. If there is anything I can do to help, please don't hesitate to let me know."

CHAPTER 10

ON THE RUN AGAIN

Callahan heard the news about Sophie's pregnancy when Jacob came to visit him. It was a blow to his self-esteem. When he and Sophie had tried unsuccessfully to conceive another child, the doctors told him that they had been unsuccessful because of some medical issues he had. They said that the couple's chance of conceiving another child was slim, and that Callahan was lucky to have Jacob. He was proud enough not to mention any of this to Sophie, much less to consider artificial insemination. Worrying whether or not Jacob was his son, he managed to send blood samples for genetic tests, making sure Sophie did not find out. He was very relieved that the tests confirmed his paternity. Now, it was evident whose fault it was.

He was yearning for some good news, but wherever he turned, the horizon looked bleak. Recently, he'd started feeling marginalized at work. Gone was the respect conveyed to him when he started his employment. It seemed that his Chinese counterparts felt that they had learned everything they needed to know from him and they no longer cared to have him around. The only reason he had not considered escaping so far was Delun's threat of harsh consequences for Jacob, who otherwise seemed very happy in California. However, Jacob, who initially liked his school, reported the recent clash between Chinese and white students and an atmosphere of fear. Callahan himself felt unsafe, as rumors spread about fearsome gangs that were traversing the country, attacking remote farms and vehicles, and stealing anything useful to them.

Callahan wondered if Delun might have a change of heart, now that he and Sophie were expecting, and help him and Jacob disappear in Central. He had heard about the assassination of Atwell and knew that the man had become a hero after his death. He had known Atwell well enough to recognize that he was no hero. He mused about the mysterious way legends are created. However, at that point, he cared more about the implication of the assassination in light of his own situation. He found out that the OD needed to deal with a populace in turmoil following the assassination, which led him to believe that the OD were no longer after him. He was no longer a threat to them, and punishing people who escaped from East, given the current circumstances, would not be a priority. But he was not sure. And besides, he was concerned that once he was in Central, people would not trust him and consider him to be a spy either for East or China. He decided to speak with Jacob about the matter next time he saw him.

Callahan felt an urge to visit the three sustainable communities he had founded in California before leaving the state. He knew that Charisma, his Southern California development, had the reputation of being an artists' and writers' village. Many people visited the place, which had become an art lover's mecca. He would love to drop by, but he knew it was too dangerous. He also wondered about Glamour, his Central Californian development, but was aware that its residents were mostly older affluent Hollywood actors, directors, producers, and writers who made sure that no unwanted visitors could even get close to their gated and highly protected village. Callahan knew that he would not be welcome there. He was hoping to go to nearby Gorgeous, another success story, but how would he find an excuse to visit without disclosing his true identity?

His wish was granted a few days later when Gorgeous's chairman called Ecological Builders, the company Callahan worked for, and asked for help with renovating their irrigation systems, as they'd made many changes to the crops they were growing since the original design. The company assigned Callahan, or Kerrigan as he was known, and two other experts to the project. True to its name, the place was gorgeous and verdant, and every inch was efficiently utilized. The people looked content and relaxed. Not glamorous, they were just no-nonsense people who lived and let live. They seemed to get along well, and their governing body seemed knowledgeable and up to the task. The initial meeting involved studying the existing system, generating some ideas, and taking measurements.

The following weekend, Callahan was on his way to his son's school. He wanted to find out the truth for himself, after having heard Jacob's fearful depiction of the situation. He knew things were deteriorating across the state, but he had not realized to what extent.

When he entered the town, he saw a roadblock. As he approached, two young white people emerged from a makeshift shack.

"What brings you to our town?" asked one of them, trying to sound friendly.

"I am going to visit my son, who goes to school here. What is going on? Are you looking for somebody?"

"Nobody in particular. We just want to make sure that no Chinese make it to town. We are trying to chase out the ones who already live here. You look okay," he said, moving the roadblock. "You can drive through."

Now Callahan understood what Jacob had been trying to tell him. He knew that many Chinese people went to school there, and many other had moved in and opened shops and other businesses. The town had become unrecognizable to its longtime residents, and the hostility of the original mostly white and Hispanic population toward the affluent newcomers seemed to have grown considerably since his last visit. Or maybe this resentment had been boiling quietly for some time and was erupting now. Whatever it was, the town looked like a harbinger of more troubles to come, and certainly not a desirable setting for a college campus.

Once Callahan reached Jacob's room, his roommate excused himself and then left to give them some privacy. "I see what you meant when we were talking during your last visit. I don't know how the state government that is mostly Chinese is going to respond to this behavior. It is not safe for anybody. I suggest that you talk to your mother and see if she can convince her husband to let both of us go. Now that she is pregnant with his child, he may grant her wish. They don't need me that much in the company anyway."

"I have already done that, Dad. She spoke with him. He is very aware of the upheaval. Mom went shopping in a store she liked, somewhat far from their gated community, and was harassed by some thugs. Delun had to come and rescue her. He is even thinking about going back to China, with her of course."

"And what about you and me?"

"I told them that you were coming. They are going to come over so we can all talk."

"Is there any way to warn them? When I drove here, I was stopped by two guys who had set up a roadblock and said they would not let any Chinese people in."

"Oh my God, it is getting worse by the minute. I will call Mom right away. I hope it's not too late." He clicked his mother's number. After a few moments, he greeted her.

"Jerome, darling, we are on our way and will be there soon. Has your dad arrived yet?"

Her rich, warm voice reminded Callahan of better days. He tried unsuccessfully to dismiss these thoughts.

"Mom, he is here. Coming from the north, he was stopped by two guys who said they are not going to let any Chinese people in. You are coming from the south, but they might have set a roadblock there too. Maybe it is not a good idea to meet here."

"Thanks for warning us. There is a Hilton with a lovely restaurant and bar about twenty miles south on the highway. If it is okay with your father, we can meet there."

James nodded in agreement, and Jacob confirmed the meeting place.

On their way to the hotel, shortly after the phone call, they saw a roadblock at the town's southern entryway. James knew that Delun Wei now owed him one.

Delun and Sonya were waiting for them in the hotel's bar. Sonya's pregnancy was impossible to ignore. Callahan could not hide the twitch of his mouth when he saw her curvy figures in a gorgeous and probably expensive light green lace dress.

Sonya looked happy and relaxed. She opened the conversation.

"Thank you for warning us and coming to meet us here. Nothing is the way it used to be. We were alarmed to hear from Jerome that he does not feel safe at school anymore. Not that we were surprised. We had some incidents ourselves. We will consider any idea you might have to improve the situation."

Looking lovingly at his wife, Delun turned to Callahan and

added, "We discussed the situation before we met you. This is my stance as well."

"I am willing to take my chances and go to Central with Jacob, or Jerome as you call him. I don't believe that he is in any danger there, but I might be. Suspicion and fear of spies exists everywhere, and in my case people might consider me a spy for East, for China, or for both. There are people in Central who hold grudges against me and might want to take revenge, using my business in the East and California against me. By the way, thanks for the raise, although if I leave, I will not be able to benefit from it."

"You are now Gene Kerrigan, not Jim Callahan. You can keep this identity," uttered Delun Wei, seemingly very surprised to hear about Callahan's reservations. "You ran away to Central in the past, remember?"

"Sure, and as you very well know, it did not go very well. You knew my identity, so I did not have to present fake degrees and letters of recommendation for Gene Kerrigan. If I hide my true identity, I will not be able to find a job or retrieve the monies in accounts owned by one James Callahan. But as I said, I am willing to take my chances."

"Very well! As far as I am concerned, you are free to go. Your coworkers told me that they feel confident they have learned from you everything there is to learn. I disagree, but under the circumstances, it is a blessing. I can fire you because of your coworkers' complaints, and then nobody will bother to follow you. You can go to Oregon and be part of Central. You don't have to visit the communities you built. I heard you were harsh on the people there. They may not like seeing you around."

Callahan was offended by the ironic tone in Delun's voice, but he knew very well that he had more reasons to worry about getting in touch with former acquaintances than Delun imagined. The Oregon idea made sense under the circumstances, although there was nothing he wanted more than to live in one of the communities he built.

"Thanks, Mr. Wei. I am waiting for a pink slip from you.

"Jacob, we can go back to your dorm and pick up your belongings. I am not sure that up north is much safer, but I would rather not have to make the trip again to pick you up."

"James, before you leave, I have a nagging question I must ask you," Sophie said. "How come our attempts to conceive another child were unsuccessful for so many years? It seems that it was not my fault."

"It was mine. The doctor told me I was lucky to have had Jacob. I was hoping for another miracle, and honestly, I was too proud to let you know about it."

"After I underwent many tests, I suspected as much. And I know that this is not the only thing you did not disclose to me. Just beware! Some of the women you treated badly may try to get even."

"Sophie, I wish we did not have to part on such a bad note, but it is what it is. Yes, I cheated on you, but I loved you very much. I wish you had discussed an escape with me. I had thought about it myself. We could have escaped together. I felt betrayed. But it all happened a long time ago. Now, I no longer feel resentment. I wish you and Delun happiness, safety, and abundance." Turning to Delun, he said, "Thanks again, Mr. Wei." Then, looking at his son, he said, "Jacob, let's go. It's getting late."

Jacob hugged his mother and thanked Delun Wei for his emotional and financial support. Then father and son departed. Back at campus, they packed Jacob's belonging as quickly as they could and then headed north. The guys who had set up the roadblock were still there, but they did not seem to care about people going out of town.

Callahan and his son hardly spoke during the two-hour drive. Jacob had not been surprised to hear about his father's cheating, because his mother ranted about it many times, especially when she tried to justify the harsh times they had gone through before she met Delun Wei. Nonetheless, Jacob was not very happy about how the conversation had turned out. Also, he felt that he would never see his mother again.

Callahan was apprehensive about the future. He felt that his trials were not over.

CHAPTER 11

THANKSGIVING

Steve was looking through the window facing the community center, beholding the last of the fall colors in the small orchard. *Another beautiful Saturday in Oasis,* he thought, mulling over possible plans to enjoy the day off with Daphne. But she called him first, and suggested that they go together to another drumming circle at Clara's.

"Sure, Daphne, I am sold," he answered, chuckling, "and I owe Clara an apology."

Once they arrived, Clara hugged both of them. Other participants were already settled in, on blankets or BackJack chairs, and smiled happily upon seeing them coming. Steve noticed that Daniel and Freda were the only other couple. The rest were women: Clara, Vanessa, Liz, and Laura.

"Before we start, are there any questions or comments?" asked Clara, glancing at Steve.

"I owe you all an apology for my hurried departure in the middle of the session last time. I did find an answer to my question about a cure for the plague, but not immediately. In the beginning, I followed the instructions and went down to the lower world. Everything was wonderful and lush as if I were in a rain forest. However, I did not meet any animal guide. I looked everywhere and asked for some guidance, but nothing happened. I gave up and decided to wait politely until the end of the drumming to tell you that I'd tried hard, but it was not for me. So, I lay still, and all of a sudden I saw the most beautiful mushroom, looking like a seductive woman dressed in a gown of psychedelic colors. She approached me and told me exactly what combination of mushrooms and herbs, all growing in my experimental garden, I needed to use and how to prepare the elixir. I had a feeling that I'd heard her telling me to administer two doses of one ounce each, one that evening and the other on the following morning. So I ran home to write it down before I forgot. Then I picked the ingredients from my garden, prepared the medicine, and drove to the hospital. I tried it on the sickest person, who seemed to be beyond cure. He improved within fifteen minutes and went to sleep, breathing steadily. Then, I administered it to all the affected patients in Faithfield Holistic Hospital and also to those in Blessed Health Hospital. I made enough for a second dose for the following day. All the patients are alive and well, and miraculously we did not see new occurrence."

"We are all happy that you found a cure, and we understand very well why you rushed out. I owe you an apology as well. I spoke about animal spirit guides because that's what most people see when they journey. However, every plant, stone, or element can be a guide. You are very dedicated to the study of plants, so it makes sense that plants would be your guides, especially given that mushrooms were part of the cure. Many *curanderos*, or healers, talk about a special relationship with plants and say that they learn from their plants what their medicinal properties are. These healers use elaborate ceremonies and don't forget to thank their guides. Have you had a similar experience with your plants, and did you remember to thank your guide?"

"I did not thank her right away, but in my heart, I thank her each day. To answer your other question, when I see my plants, I always know if they have any deficiency. My lab tests just confirm it. I don't think I had any insight into a cure. I have studied and experimented with my plants, but I never thought that I could receive an answer to my questions from them. When I published an article about the preparation and use of the medication, I included a lot of the details of my prior research and tried to develop a theory about why it all works together. I decided to be somewhat honest and mentioned that I had learned some of the details from a dream. Obviously, I could not mention that I received the information from a mushroom during a shamanic drumming session."

Everybody laughed heartily.

"You actually were fairly honest, Steve, since journeying is going into the dream world. Besides, people make discoveries as a result of various unintentional events: an apple falls, a mistake leads to an unexpected result, and probably many inventors dreamed of their inventions. However, you would have never dreamed it if you had not put all the work into cultivating your garden and studying your plants. After all, the plants were all there; you just had to pick the right ones and prepare and administer the elixir properly.

"Before I start drumming, I want to reiterate that you may meet the guide or guides you met before, or some new ones. Just be open and let things happen. Also, it is a good idea to have a journal where you can write down your experience. Stanly is busy today; therefore, I will drum."

Fifteen minutes later, they were all jotting some notes in their journals. After a short pause, Clara asked if they had any questions or wanted to share their experiences.

"Unlike my previous journeys, this one was very frightening. I was led by my guide to a mountaintop, where I saw carnage. Everything was covered in blood. The face of humanity was that of hate and fear," said Liz. "My intent was to find out what is going to happen in the future and how to handle it. I guess I received an answer to the 'what' question, not the 'how.'"

"That's strange," responded Clara. "I had an unusually scary journey too. I wonder if others had the same experience." Three participants raised their hands.

"We should brace ourselves for a hard time. It does not mean we should be scared. It means we need to get together and start thinking about protection. I will talk with Stanly about the need to get together and speak about it. I will also ask Rudolph to give us the latest information on climate change and what is happening politically."

"I hope that your grim mood will change by Thanksgiving dinner next week. We are all working hard to make it a memorable experience. And we have a lot to be thankful for," noted Daphne.

Daphne accompanied Steve to his home. They had lunch together.

"Steve, did you have a great revelation this time as well?"

"Today I did not seek an answer to any burning medical or therapeutic questions, and I did not meet the mushroom either. I saw a masculine guide. I asked about our relationship. You see, never in my life did I think I would be involved with an actress or any other celebrity. I love you. How can I not love you? You are the most wonderful woman I have ever met. I wish you were less famous. I needed to know if I can trust you." Steve looked embarrassed.

Daphne said softly, "You are very famous as well, not only because you are a frequent guest on my show, but also because you found a cure for the plague. Anyway, I asked about our relationship as well. I have my issues with men—none of which are your fault. But I have trust issue too. When I journeyed, I was encouraged to work harder on our relationship. We need to be more open with each other. It seems that we are both on guard. We are good friends and have a great time in and out of bed, but we know virtually nothing about each other. And nowadays, trust is more important than ever."

"You are right, Daphne. I feel the same way. So who is going to start?"

"I will, but can I get a glass of wine first, please?"

"Sure, Daphne. I kept a good bottle just for this occasion," Steve said, smiling warmly. He went to the pantry to retrieve the bottle. He picked up a champagne glass, filled it with the red liquid, and put it in front of Daphne.

Daphne took a sip of her drink, set her elbows on the table, rested her face on her clasped hands, and sighed.

She spoke about her unhappy childhood. Her alcoholic father abused her mother and used to beat her and her sister when he came home drunk, lost his job, or was just in a bad mood. Finally, he disappeared when she was about twelve. Although they were very poor, they felt better with him gone. Unfortunately, their relief did not last long. Two years later, her mother married a man who had looked okay when they were dating. But after their wedding, he was even worse than Daphne's father. Daphne started crying, but she forced herself to continue.

"Not only did he beat everybody when he was drunk, but he also raped me more than once. I told the social worker at school, and they removed me from the home and placed me with my aunt. I would have never finished school if it hadn't been for her. My mother eventually divorced this monster to protect my sister.

"I loved acting. I took some classes and was lucky to find some jobs in movies and commercials. I accepted every job offered to me, which enabled me to buy this home. However, I don't like the limelight. I have always lived away from Hollywood parties and other sensations. I find it hard to work in the theater too.

"My love life was not spectacular either. I did not have many intimate relationships, and the ones I had were terrible. I lost hope and decided to live my life by myself, developing myself to become what I wanted to become. Then, you showed up in my life."

"I am glad I did. And thank you for sharing, Daphne. Whatever happens between us, I will always be frank and never hurt you." He got up, hugged her, and then returned to his seat.

"My turn, I guess," he said softly.

He related that his childhood had not been happy either, although he was not abused or beaten. His family was very poor as well. His dad worked hard and most of the times returned home exhausted. Then he just watched his favorite shows on the communication device, read the news, and wanted nothing to do with Steve or his brother. The man died of a heart attack when Steve was sixteen. Steve's depressed mother was on one antidepressant or another, and she was not very caring either. Steve believed that her depression was at least partially responsible for his dad's remoteness and possibly his early death.

Continuing with his story, Steve related to Daphne that he had always dreamed of being a doctor. He knew that if he wanted to achieve that end, he had to have good grades and lots of money. Consequently, he worked hard at school and tried to make as much as money as he could, money that he hid from his family. He put himself through college by attending one that was close to home and reasonably good, and after graduating he was accepted to medical school. He even was awarded some scholarships, but still he had to take some loans to pay for his studies.

He continued by telling Daphne how he had pursued herbal medicine and nutrition and had taken as many classes as he could in these areas in spite of the objection of his supervising doctors, and in spite of the fact that he was working in two hospitals seven days a week, twelve hours a day, to pay his rent and student loans.

"Anyway, it is strange that I care about people so much but have no close friends. I could never find the time to develop relationships. So, when Charlotte showed up in my life, I was hoping that was it. She is a nurse and very efficient at everything she does, so I thought she'd be able to help in my practice. Of course, she is an attractive woman as well. However, I can live with many imperfections, but not with betrayal. I realized it when I drove like a nut to bring her back from Sanctuary when she asked me to, just to find out that I will never trust her again. I am happy she is engaged to Dr. Salerno and moved in with him and his kids. Then I met you …"

"Steve, I will always be honest with you and never betray you. Do you have any family around?"

"My mother died shortly before I finished my residency. My younger brother was nothing like me. He hated school and always dreamed of playing in a band. He has a pleasant voice, can write lyrics that his audience likes, and has mastered a few musical instruments. We have never been close. When I went to school, he moved from one band to another. I have no clue if he is dead or alive. I don't know how to find him, and I doubt that he is aware that I live here. How about your family?"

"I am originally from the East Coast. My mother and younger sister have moved around but are still in East. Now it is hard for them to leave, but if they succeed, they know where to find me. I made peace with my mother. It was not easy, but I did. If they show up, I will do my best to help them settle. I just hope that they are hanging in there."

Daphne and Steve moved to the living room sofa and held each other tight.

"Daphne, will you marry me?"

"I will, Steve."

"We will announce it at the Thanksgiving dinner!"

◆◆◆◆◆◆

Steve and Daphne were looking forward to having a lovely Thanksgiving dinner, trying not to think about potential natural or human-made disasters. They contemplated telling their community about their upcoming marriage. Like the rest of the residents, they provided ingredients and volunteered to do some cooking and cleaning up. That is, Steve donated some of his tastiest esoteric plants, and Daphne volunteered to cook them following his instructions. Daphne organized the decoration of the dining room and took care of the artistic part of the program, ensuring that the local musicians would demonstrate their talents and the schoolchildren would perform a Thanksgiving play.

On Thanksgiving Day, they put on their good clothes, walked to the center, and joined their friends around the table covered with beautiful dishes, filling their plates and complimenting the cooks.

The ceremony commenced with an emotional speech by Stanly, thanking all for the amazing, affluent, safe community they had contributed to creating, and for their contribution to the well-being of people outside the community. He invited everybody, including the children to briefly share what they were thankful for. The children, who had rehearsed their mini speeches but still were embarrassed to speak in public, thanked their families and expressed thanks for the community school and the food they were eating. The adults were thankful to have found a safe and friendly shelter in Oasis, and were also grateful for the food, their families, and the beautiful ceremony. When it was his turn to speak, Steve said that he was thankful for having been able to find a cure for the terrible disease. "Most of all I am grateful that I asked Daphne to marry me, and she said yes."

Everybody clapped and cheered happily.

Daphne, who was sitting next to Steve, expressed her thanks for the proposal as well as for her successful weekly show that helped the viewers to live sustainably.

Everybody enjoyed Stanly playing the piano as he accompanied Sarah, Rudolph's wife, who had been "discovered" as having a charming voice. Stanly played a duet with Judy who played the violin. The children's play was cute. In the end, everybody helped with cleanup and were thankful for a peaceful, joyous evening.

Three weeks later, Oasis celebrated the wedding of Daphne and Steve. Nobody could overlook the small baby bump. Steve was happy, although somewhat apprehensive about bringing a child into the world under such circumstances. Daphne moved in with him and thereafter used only her beautiful office/showroom in her own home. The rest would be used by her mother and sister when they arrived. There was no question in her mind that they would come.

CHAPTER 12

THE RETALIATION

Arnold Oliphant was stunned to hear about Atwell's assassination. Although he had not liked Atwell's latest efforts to improve people's lives, he knew that Atwell, being afraid for his safety, would obey him once he ordered him to stop the planned welfare programs. Oliphant was very aware that he was indebted to Atwell for the institution of OD rule over the entire East. Even though he was concerned when Atwell seemed reluctant to command an invasion of Central, he'd been hoping to work out something to uplift his spirit and commit him to action. Now that Atwell was dead, such a thing was impossible. And it was clear that Oliphant's decision to send a missile to Central had been prematurely made. He could not blame it on Atwell, and he needed to find a way to appease Hickman. But what bothered Oliphant most was the question of who had ordered this assassination, because it certainly wasn't him.

Oliphant had already sent Terry, his confidant, to investigate who was behind the murder. Many times in the past he had ordered his executors to "take care" of people who threatened the OD, either because of their lack of loyalty or their inefficiency, but never before had somebody dared to execute someone as important as a president without receiving an explicit order from him. Oliphant felt that the control Atwell had worked so hard to obtain would now crumble as a result of the assassination. And if that were not enough, Atwell had become a martyr and a hero, with no one believing that he had died of a stroke. Hence Oliphant needed to find the people behind the murder and execute them publicly so as to appease the angry masses.

For the time being, Oliphant had to let the vice president, Norris Gunderson, serve as president. He knew that Gunderson and Atwell had not gotten along well and that Atwell marginalized Gunderson and would not let him participate in any important decision. When he nominated Gunderson two years ago, Oliphant thought it was a brilliant move that would ensure that he would learn of any possible noncompliance by Atwell. Now he regretted his choice and was quite sure that Gunderson was behind the murder. All he could do was to go with the stroke as the official cause of death, promise a thorough autopsy, and give an emotional speech praising the late president.

The fact that Sarah and the children had run away as soon as they found out about Atwell's death endangered the credibility of the entire regime. Even more terrifying was the thought that Atwell might have shared with his wife some information about the location of the Hub. If he had, then the OD were no longer safe. Oliphant moved his family out of the Hub just in case, but he could not imagine how he could evacuate all the families who lived there, along with the offices and the arsenal.

Ten days after the assassination, Oliphant received the final autopsy report. Atwell had been assassinated by an electric wave delivered in his office, probably from the ceiling. As Oliphant was reading the report, Terry, his confidant, arrived, seemingly shaky and agitated.

"I don't like what I encountered there. Everybody seemed scared and afraid to talk. Gunderson said flatly that he knew nothing and doubted it was an assassination. Norma, Atwell's aide, confided that on the day of the murder, rumors circulated throughout the office that the OD had ordered Atwell's assassination. She said she was saddened but not surprised by his death. Norma looked confused and troubled when I mentioned that no such order had been given. She refused to name suspects. I gave her my card, with instructions on how to contact me safely, and promised a financial reward if she came up with some helpful information. It seems that she will be able to obtain the info if she tries. Nobody else was genuinely cooperating. It appears that whoever planned the murder also disseminated the rumors about the ordered assassination. And people believed it. People are afraid to point fingers. We have some inner-circle individuals who are connected to different cliques and are reporting what people are saying. So far, they have not gotten any more information than I have already related to you. One of these people, an attractive woman who works in close collaboration with Gunderson, will try to get a confession if she can, but so far she has no evidence that he is involved. Also, everybody is concerned about the unrest."

Oliphant thanked Terry and asked him to report any new development. He knew that the only way to counter the rumor of an OD-ordered assassination was by starting a counter-rumor. Upon his order, his people circulated the rumor that Gunderson was behind the murder, the motive being that Gunderson hated Atwell and coveted the presidency. Oliphant would have loved to have real evidence, but he knew he could fabricate some if need be. He called Jeff, the commander of the OD mercenary army. Knowing that the regular army was now under Gunderson's control and therefore could not be trusted, Oliphant ordered Jeff to assume the role of maintainer of order and told him to be ready to assassinate Gunderson if necessary.

The buzz about Gunderson being behind the murder went viral, and people seemed to buy into it. Gunderson created a counter-rumor that he was afraid that the OD would do to him what they had done to Atwell, and that's why they were spreading the rumors about him.

People were confused. Government employees sensed the war that was going on between Gunderson and the OD and tried to stay out of it. Oliphant knew he had no time to lose. He ordered the mercenaries to arrest Gunderson for treason and murder and then to place him in a maximum-security prison. The mercenaries managed to arrest Gunderson. They put his wife and son under house arrest to make sure they did not escape like their predecessors.

Then a teary-eyed Oliphant appeared on the communications system and reiterated how saddened he was when he'd found out about Atwell's death. He recounted the great, unmatchable contributions Atwell had made to ensure prosperity in the East. Oliphant apologized for the initial broadcast announcing that Atwell had died of a stroke, explaining that it had seemed like the most logical explanation to disseminate at the time, while they were waiting for the autopsy result. He continued by admitting that most people rightfully did not believe the initial report and saying that the autopsy had revealed the cause of death to be electric shock. On top of that, he told the populace that the investigators had found a device capable of delivering an electric shock in a vent just above Atwell's Oval office. He concluded by saying that Gunderson was the main suspect and was already under arrest, and promised a due process. Then, he let the media interview the physicians who had performed the autopsy, the technical team that had discovered the device above Atwell's office, and coworkers who could testify to the hostility between Gunderson and Atwell.

***

David was on his way to Colorado, reflecting on the last meeting of the Geek Clique, the small group of MIT graduates who had started organizing secretly in Cambridge in preparation for the meeting with Atwell. After the meeting they were hopeful, believing that there might be a way to work something out with the regime to improve people's living conditions without resorting to violence. They were thinking about creative methods to ensure enough food shelter and energy for all. Atwell's death had made it clear that this was not going to happen, regardless of who was truly behind the assassination. Moreover, they suspected that Atwell's attempt to collaborate with people outside the OD circle might have had something to do with his death. Since many of the clique members lived in Prosperity, the community Callahan had developed in the Northeast, they could easily convene secretly and conduct experiments in their basements. They were sure that given their training they would figure out how to produce and deliver explosives to the OD Hub once they knew where the target was.

The group had decided to send David to meet with Governor Hickman and offer the group's help in toppling the OD. Simultaneously, other members would start developing explosives that, when the time was right, could be used against the OD. David's job was to convince Hickman that they were able to do the job, if given the appropriate information and possibly some support.

And not only could they destroy the Hub, but also they created a task force to plan for what would happen once they'd succeeded in overthrowing the OD, the aim being to prevent chaos. Among other things, they had started identifying talented and honest people to govern East until they could establish general elections.

David took a big risk going to Colorado, one based on a very slim hope that somebody with knowledge of the location of the mysterious OD Hub had succeeded in escaping to Central, or alternatively that Hickman would assist the group if such person could not be found. David and his fellow geeks assumed that everybody in Central would gladly help them get rid of the OD now that a missile had been launched against them. They also assumed that in Central, as in East, nobody believed that the Russians had sent this missile. But these were risky assumptions; the members of the Geek Clique were well aware that any mistake in disclosing the plan to the wrong person would mean a death sentence for all of them.

Now, David had left the group behind and was all by himself on the road. The group had collected money to buy him a stealth, auto-driven car, a fake ID, and the huge mustache glued to his face, which was otherwise clean-shaven. They'd done everything they could to make sure he would not be caught by the OD, or that if—God forbid—he was caught, nothing would connect him with the group, their friends, or their families. Approaching his fortieth birthday, David was still a bachelor, although he had a girlfriend, who knew nothing about his trip. Neither did his old parents. He told nobody, but he was ready to commit suicide if seized by the OD.

So far David had not used the stealth mode, preserving it for the time when he would cross the Mississippi into Central. Moving his hand through his thick, curly hair, he checked the detector and noticed a drone flying just over the car. To be safe, he entered a covered garage next to an office building and emerged from the other side in stealth mode. He left the highway and drove onto a side road. After being satisfied that the danger had passed, he changed back to the highway. At night, he used the stealth ferry used by refugees, for a considerable fee, when escaping to freedom. Only when he reached the other side did he allow himself to sleep, trusting that his beeper would wake him should something unexpected happen.

Once in Denver, David contacted the governor's office, presented himself as the Geek Clique emissary, and after submitting to a thorough security check of his body and his car was let in.

Governor Adam Hickman received him respectfully, but he kept his lips sealed as far as providing him with useful information went. Although he'd requested a comprehensive background check on David and the Geek Clique and was satisfied that they were trustworthy, he could not tell David about Central's plans to combat the OD without compromising those plans. Also, he was not sure what a bunch of geeks were capable of doing and believed that the OD would more likely eliminate them than vice versa. However, he thought that local allies might be helpful in providing last-minute info when Central decided to act.

So, Hickman told David that Central was mulling over some plans to retaliate, providing no details and saying nothing about the map. With a fatherly tone, he urged David and his friends to be very careful. He added that at this point, he could only give them the name of one person in the Northeast to serve as a liaison when needed.

David, aware that he was being mistrusted and misled, was disappointed. He sensed that Hickman knew much more than he'd disclosed. Not willing to return empty-handed, David asked nonchalantly who this person was.

"Her name is Riva Davis, and her phone number is six one seven, nine nine eight, nine nine seven one. Introduce yourself as Dr. Center and ask to meet her."

David entered the number into his system and uttered, "It can't be!"

"Something wrong?"

"Yes, indeed! I have this number in my system. It belongs to a man, not a woman, and his last name is not Davis."

It was Hickman's turn to be surprised. He left David in the office and ran out to double-check the number with his assistant. She confirmed the number and added that she had spoken with Riva a week ago. David insisted that the number belonged to a colleague at MIT whom he knew very well but who was not part of the clique.

"We do not want him in Geek Clique. He has done a lot of research for the OD, and we do not trust him."

Hickman dropped his paternal demeanor and looked genuinely worried. "How much does Riva know?" he asked his assistant.

"She does not know about any of the plans, but she knows about the map."

The assistant was searching frantically in her information system.

"David is right. The phone belongs to MIT professor Roger Lewandowski. He might have masked his voice, because it sounded very feminine to me."

"Is he married? What is the name of his significant other?" asked Hickman, hanging on his last hope.

"He was married, and his wife disappeared under mysterious circumstances. He does have a mistress, his very attractive lab assistant. I don't know her very well, but I would not trust her either."

"We have to act fast, and we will need your help, David. We know their location, and we have a delivery system. We will need your help for feedback. I will give you a copy of the map that is visible only after a specific chemical treatment is applied. We will also give you a code for communicating with us. Use an unassigned communications system, preferably from a Central-controlled area. D-Day is Thanksgiving Day. Be safe."

It took David three days to return home, and it seemed that his stealth car had not been detected by the OD. Thanksgiving was only two days away. To his surprise, he received an invitation to have Thanksgiving dinner at the home of Professor Lewandowski. He declined politely, mentioning plans to celebrate with family. He made the map visible and learned the codebook but did not inform the group, presuming that the fewer people who knew, the better. He assumed that any possible hit from Central, on target or not, would be reported, and then he would have to figure out the location of the hit and report back. He tried not to think about the strange Thanksgiving dinner invitation he'd received from Lewandowski.

The Geek Clique planned to get together for a leftovers potluck on Friday following Thanksgiving Day to hear about David's trip, unsuspecting of the upcoming plan.

Unbeknown to them, another rebel group, the Freedom Fighters, had their own plans for Thanksgiving. They'd obtained the map from

Arthur, Atwell's driver, before he'd been caught and executed by the OD. The group consisted ten people with diverse backgrounds. One of them, Serge, supervised delivering goods to the OD Hub. Although he did not know the exact location of the Hub, Serge did know the timing and content of the shipments carried by driverless trucks that were programmed to reach the Hub. The Freedom Fighters' plan was to plant some explosives amid the cargo and deliver that cargo to the venue of the OD Thanksgiving dinner.

Many people bit their nails during Thanksgiving Day. David, who celebrated with his parents, monitored his communications system all day. If the broadcasting system reported nothing by the evening, he would call a friend who lived not far from the Hub area to find out if he had noticed anything unusual.

The family finished the festive meal around 2:00 p.m. and still David had heard nothing. So, he decided to drive home before nightfall. Just as he was about to set out, he heard the sirens of OD secret service vehicles. *I had better wait and see what it's all about,* he thought. About half an hour later, a short message appeared on the communications system.

"A cargo truck containing explosives crashed into a residence in the mountains of eastern Pennsylvania. Ten people are dead, and twenty people, injured and in various conditions, were taken to a nearby hospital. The police have arrested five people connected to this hideous terrorist act, and we are going to punish the offenders and their families severely. The names are Serge Gorki, Arlene Dugan, John Shuler, Miranda Munoz, and Henry Wise. People who know any of these five criminals are invited to come forward and provide information to support the investigation. Any person providing useful information will be rewarded."

David started shaking and struggled to prevent vomiting. He did not know any of the people mentioned in the report, but he could imagine what would have happened if it had been his group. Assuming that they were trying to hit the Hub, located in the general area according to the map Hickman had showed him, the results were not worthy of their sacrifice.

That cannot be what Hickman had in mind. Probably something went wrong and they canceled the plan.

David kissed his parents and drove home, planning to follow a number of news sources to get a clearer picture of the event. A message on his messenger device announced the cancellation of the Friday leftovers party. David was relieved. His friends could not help him now, so he had better not get them involved. Feeling that he was on his own, as any attempt to share would put others in harm's way, he decided not to call his friend in Pennsylvania. But once at home, he dropped into his bed flat on his back and just stared at the ceiling, unable to think coherently.

Apparently he fell asleep, because suddenly he felt as if he was flying off his bed.

What is going on? Am I going mad? He jumped to his feet and felt another jolt. *I am not dreaming; it appears to be an earthquake. It cannot be the result of a missile from Central; we are too far! Or can it?*

David opened the shutters and saw many people in the street. He checked the communications system but found no reference to the event. He was on his way to join the crowd outside when the phone rang.

"David, this is Ed from Pennsylvania. I have to ask you for a huge favor. An enormous explosion about fifty miles from here has caused havoc all around. Some people say they saw missiles flying from the west. They probably hit an underground OD armory. It must be huge, because many ambulances are rushing from there to nearby hospitals. In my neighborhood, many homes are damaged. My house has cracks, and I don't think it's safe. I suspect that the air quality resulting from the fire and explosions is unhealthy, to say the least. I have no other place to go. Can I stay with you for a while?"

"Sure, buddy, that's what friends are for. I felt an earthquake-like jolt here in Cambridge and could not figure out what it was. Do you think it might be related to this explosion?"

"Oh my God, you are three hundred miles away! Is your home safe?"

"Yes, don't worry! You have a long drive. Pack as many clothes food and necessities as you can load, and then get going. You can tell me everything after your arrival. Good luck!"

David looked at the posts appearing on his communication device. *I don't think Hickman needs my feedback. All he has to do is read the posts.*

CHAPTER 13

COMING HOME

James and Jacob Callahan, who had gone back to using their original names, arrived home after a long drive. They were planning to move out of California as soon as Delun fired James. James started packing as much as he could into the good old motor home, but he continued going to work as if the conversation with Sophie and Delun had never happened.

James did not have to wait too long. He knew that Delun was a man of his word and would fire him as soon as he could get approval to do so. Two weeks later, a letter of dismissal was handed to Callahan by his team leader, who did not hide his satisfaction about seeing him going. The following day, father and son were on their way to Oregon. They noticed that nobody seemed to care about them leaving or attempted to stop them.

James knew he had to watch his expenses until he could secure employment, so he found an inexpensive RV parking area just south of Eugene. He was not thrilled to connect his vehicle to the utilities and join the climate refugees who traveled across the country in search of employment, but he thought of this situation as temporary. Although he had never worked in Oregon before and had no connections there, Callahan, given his reputation, was hoping to be hired for a project designing or repairing new homes shortly.

Callahan was looking for a job, but it did not seem that people were eager to hire him. From places where he applied, he'd received either polite rejections or no answer at all. His pride was the victim of this failure, even more than his checkbook. He felt alienated, lost, and old. He wanted to go home, but where was home?

Jacob was not happy either. The young man who took after his mother was lightly built and lacked the confidence his father had in abundance. He admired his father and lived in his shadow. Now, he was very troubled. Just as he had gotten used to his stepfather, who'd assumed financial responsibility for his college studies, and felt that his life was finally on the right track, his birth father showed up and his mother got pregnant. So, once again he felt like a stranger in his mother and stepfather's home, and he didn't feel fully at home with his father, especially now that his famously self-confident father seemed broken and dejected, was preoccupied with his problems, and paid little attention to his son.

With dread, Jacob remembered traveling around with his mother when she was trying to settle in Central, unable to find a job or a partner who could support her, and felt a sense of déjà vu. So, he decided to find a job, any job, to earn his own money. He was not as picky as his father. He took a variety of odd jobs and did make some money, but he felt lonely and forlorn. He made no friends among his coworkers. His daydreams about meeting a lovely girl and being "adopted" by her family were nothing but dreams. In reality, no one showed even the slightest interest in him. He remembered fondly his college girlfriend, whom he probably would never see again. His love life was also a casualty of his current situation.

Thanksgiving Day arrived, and neither Jacob nor James felt very thankful. They decided to participate in an inexpensive celebration in a two-star hotel, but it did not improve their mood. To the contrary, being surrounded by lonely people who were not sure where their next meal was coming from just increased their gloom.

The following day as they ate breakfast in their camper, they heard, as did the rest of the country, about the missiles that had hit the Hub of the Order Defenders, and about OD members fleeing the country. James's dark mood changed into a sense of relief and joy.

"I am free at last. The OD are not going to look for me anymore. They have more important things to worry about," he told Jacob. His mind was mulling over the next steps.

He knew there were two phone calls he needed to make. First, he would call Governor Adam Hickman, whom he'd met well before the disasters, when he built the Oasis, Refuge, and Sanctuary communities in Colorado. They'd become friends, and their wives grew very close. Sophie hated James for moving to the East because she loved Denver and had a satisfying teaching job and many friends besides Hickman's wife, Dara. Callahan was hoping that Hickman would offer him a job for the sake of the good old days.

He introduced himself to Hickman's secretary as an old friend, and she connected him with the governor.

"Good morning, James! Last time I heard about you, you were living in the East working hand in hand with the Order Defenders. Where are you now?"

"I am in Oregon and plan to settle in Colorado. It is a long story," he said, giving the governor a short version of his adventures.

"Colorado is a free state, and you are welcome to use your skills whatever way you wish. If you happen to stop in Denver, give me a call. I would love to hear about your adventures. Oh, I am sorry that Sophie is not coming with you, because I am sure that Dara would have liked to meet her."

Callahan bit his lip. He realized that Hickman did not trust him and would not consider him for any job. But he was the governor of Colorado and the center of the coalition of the willing, so James had better accept the invitation.

"Thanks, Governor. I would love to tell you everything I know about the East and the West. There is a good chance that I will be in Denver soon, as I plan to visit Oasis and Sanctuary. I will contact you when I get there."

"Good luck, James."

The second call Callahan needed to make was to Clara. He punched Clara's number. Hearing her line ringing, he was wondering how she would treat him now that her sister was married to a different man. He also wondered how he would be received in Oasis, as many residents believed he had treated them harshly.

"Hi, Clara. It is James Callahan. I hope you still remember me."

"Of course I remember you. I hope you are okay after those missiles fell on your Hub. I am sorry to tell you that I have not heard from my sister and have had no clue as to her whereabouts for very long time."

Callahan repeated the story he'd told Hickman, adding the news about Sophie's pregnancy and asked if he could visit Oasis. He also asked how everybody was doing.

"James, are you serious about Sophie?"

"Unfortunately, yes. You will be able to verify it with Jacob when we come to visit."

"Of course you can visit, but there is nowhere for you to stay, unless you have a motor home that you can park here and connect to water and electricity. I just want to warn you that the lots you owned were legally transferred to Oasis ownership as payment for the unfinished community center. We did build the community center, and we are thriving. Most of the original people are still here. I am not sure they will be glad to see you. The farmer who bought from you ran away. His wife remarried, and her second husband was arrested by Intelligence for treason. Charlotte is no longer with Steve, and no longer in Oasis either, and Steve and Daphne got married. Did I answer all your questions?"

"Pretty much, Clara," responded Callahan in a disheartened voice. He had hope for a warmer invitation. "I will see you soon."

They hung up.

"Jacob, we are going to Colorado! If you help me with the driving, we can be there in two days."

"Are we headed to Denver? Did Hickman offer you a job?" asked Jacob, who had overheard some of the conversation.

"We are going first to Denver and then to Oasis. Hickman did not offer me any job, Son. People do not trust me, and it would be a challenge to change that. I am not sure where I am going to settle, and it is not fair to you to drag you along with me. I will try to establish myself in Oasis though. I have some money in the Oasis bank and hope that it will pay for your college studies. There is a nice small university in Faithfield that I think you would like. It is about half an hour from Oasis, so you will be close to your aunt in case I have to move on. If you don't like it, you can check what is available in Denver."

"Thanks, Dad," responded Jacob. James noticed the young man's gloom change to joy. *He is happy to go back to school and probably does not care if I am around or not,* thought James.

After two long days traveling, they reached an RV park near Denver. Callahan contacted Governor Hickman, who was surprised to hear that he was already in Denver, but he was friendly and suggested a private lunch for the two of them.

Callahan looked at the mirror, trying to see himself through the eyes of a person who had known him in his heyday as a successful developer. Since that time, he had grown an unkempt beard and long hair. His clothes, once made by famous designers, were now cheap and old. He did not care about the change. Actually, he felt safer and more like himself being somewhat shabby and hiding behind an unassuming appearance that did not attract much attention. He just wondered if the governor would recognize him. So, he picked the best clothes he could find, did his best to groom his wild beard, and went to meet Hickman.

Hickman could not hide his surprise upon seeing the current version of Callahan, but he quickly rebounded, smiling and giving him a warm handshake. "Good to see you! I ordered a tasty lunch for both of us in my office, where we can have a private talk."

The food was served as soon as they entered the office. Then Hickman closed the door and asked his secretary not to disturb him unless it was an emergency.

"I will be honest with you, James. We heard about your work for the Order Defenders. I did not expect you to be an angel, but I need to understand why you collaborated with them. You see, we accepted refugees from East without asking too many questions, just trying to make sure they were not spies. I cannot reject you as a resident, but I am honestly trying to understand."

"I am not an angel, but I am not an evil person. As you know, following the disasters, the government was in disarray and did not provide any help. It could not even stop the gangs that traversed the land and killed anybody who refused to give them everything they wanted. Then the OD appeared, presenting themselves as angels who had come to help these miserable people. We all trusted them because we wanted to believe.

When they hired me, I felt like a hero who comes to the rescue. I did not like the communities they designed, but I assumed they did not provide something better because of budget constraints. So, I worked hard at nights to develop a better plan, with somewhat larger units and lots for growing food. I proudly presented the plan to Oliphant, the OD chairman, but he just laughed dryly and threw it into the wastebasket. He told me flatly that the OD were not interested in making the lives of these people better. Later, I, as everybody else in East, found that the 'help' they'd provided was all part of a scheme to enslave the people they'd rescued and force them to work for minimum wage in the OD factories and on the OD farms. Then, it was hard to get away."

"Oliphant. Is it by any chance Arnold Oliphant? I had a friend from college named Oliphant, and I heard that he made a fortune from a Wall Street hedge fund. He is the second guy from the left, in the back row," said Hickman, pointing to a framed picture of a football team hanging on the wall.

Callahan got up and approached the photograph.

"Yep, that's him, the devil incarnate."

"I don't understand. Here in Central, we have never heard anything about him. If he was that powerful, why didn't he become the president?"

"The OD did not want people to know who was behind their misery. So they picked other people to be the façade for the regime without giving them too much power. The OD had their mercenary army, sophisticated arsenals, and all the money. The president received a small budget and the number of military troops necessary to keep law and order. Atwell was not one of the OD, and neither was Gunderson. Nor was I. Atwell served them well, and I suspect that Gunderson, who hated his guts, was the one behind his assassination, not the OD. But many other civil servants who displeased the OD in one way or another disappeared, and we were told that they had been taken care of. Needless to say, we lived amid an atmosphere of fear and suspicion."

"But you did escape, didn't you?"

Callahan reiterated his escape story and told Hickman how he'd been kidnapped while sleeping in a friend's home.

"Just out of curiosity, what is the name of your friend in Austin?"

"Tom Vargas. He left home for work, but the Chinese kidnapped me before he came back home. I wonder if he or one of those friends he'd asked to visit with me betrayed me. I hate to think that Tom might have …"

"I had the feeling you would mention a familiar name. He is one of ten men convicted in Texas of spying for the OD. How did you befriend him?"

"He was my college roommate and a great guy. I don't believe he was a spy. Maybe his friends in Intelligence were. And I was kidnapped by the Chinese, not the OD."

"One of them, not Vargas, spied for both the OD and the Chinese. The Chinese just acted faster."

"I still cannot believe it! Anyway, can I talk with him and hear his version?"

"I am afraid you will never be able to see him again."

Now, Callahan was not a very sentimental guy, but the memories of him partying with his friend with the prettiest women on campus and of their long conversations did leave him teary-eyed.

"I am sorry. I was not involved in the trial, but the pictures appeared on all the communication devices." Hickman searched his computer and projected a picture onto the wall. Callahan nodded, confirming the identity of his friend and feeling that there was no place safe for him in the world anymore.

A pensive Hickman noted, "I still find it hard to believe your story about the enslaving of the disaster refugees. I thought we abandoned slavery a long time ago. And how did the OD succeed in gaining such a hold over people in the land of the free?"

"Governor, we abandoned slavery as a legal system of exploitation for the purpose of obtaining cheap labor, but we found other ways to do the same thing in a more morally palatable way. Think about getting cheap labor by outsourcing to Third World countries, and exploitation of illegal immigrants here. The OD did not describe the system as slavery, just as a method of repaying mortgage debts, but for all practical purposes it was the same. You are probably aware that they acquired control of the energy, food, and medical industries. The lack of any of these is one of people's deepest fears. Exploiting this fear made it easier for the OD to control people in times of shortage and crisis. You see, they are the climate change deniers who contributed to the disasters, and they are the ones benefiting from the results. They were behind the development of genetically engineered food using toxic fertilizers, knowing very well how harmful they are, and they are the ones who are behind the medical and pharmaceutical industries that profit from having more sick people to whom to sell services and thereby be able to control."

"Hmm, you sound cynical, but I see your point. I heard that the Illuminati were fleeing the East. Do you believe that it's all over?"

"I am not sure. I heard rumors about a chasm among the Illuminati or OD as we call them now. Some of them objected to Oliphant's leadership and tried to live inconspicuously, hiding their legendary wealth. They probably stayed. I don't know much about them or what to expect. Many of them may live incognito in Central and have their ways of sending communications without the messages being intercepted. We should keep our eyes open. Your question makes me think that they might be behind Atwell's assassination, rather than Gunderson or the OD."

"Very interesting. Thank you for your observations and insight. If you can, please tell me about your Chinese experience."

After hearing about Callahan's adventures, all Hickman could say was, "Wow! I don't know why, but I do believe your story. I am not sure about other people, though. You will have a lot of explaining to do. Please keep in touch. We may need your familiarity with East and California to help us understand how events unfold there."

"I will. Thanks for lunch, and even more for your trust."

The following day, James and Jacob arrived at Oasis. Clara invited them to dinner but did not ask them to stay with her and her husband. There were a lot of questions, and in response Callahan repeated the same stories he'd told Hickman. Knowing Clara, he also mentioned his experience at the Miwok ceremony, but she did not soften her gaze. Callahan asked many questions about Oasis and the other two Central communities. Both Clara and Stanly emphasized how great Oasis was doing even though Callahan had left them with an unfinished community center. They told him that they'd heard only stories of mistrust and fear about Sanctuary. Since Edna, Clara's other sister, lived in Refuge, they were able to share with Callahan that the community was thriving, but the relationship between residents were not as close as those in Oasis since the people of Refuge preferred to do business and entertain themselves in the adjacent town, not with each other. So, they had no school or factory, and fewer social activities were taking place at the community center. That was enough to convince Callahan that he should do his best to be part of the Oasis community.

Before leaving, Callahan asked Clara half-jokingly, and not without sarcasm, "After what I have told you, do you still believe that the human race is evolving?"

"It depends on what you mean by 'evolving.' If you define it as a sudden genetic change or some other change implanted in the human race by God or other celestial beings, something that somehow would change the entire human race or keep the righteous people and purge the evil ones, then the answer is no. I don't believe that the Messiah is coming anytime soon. I did not hold my breath in 2012, when I was fifteen, or any other time when evolutionary change was predicted. Come to think about it, I assume that when we evolved from the apes, not all the apes evolved, and the first human had to survive in a very hostile world filled with, among other creatures, apes.

"However, I do believe that some of our youngsters are more developed than we are. I know that both of my girls, but Sue in particular, can sense and understand people, issues, and events much better and at a younger age than I. When I was young, many people who were different and could not function in their reality were labeled as mentally ill and were sedated, so I did not believe that they were going to save the world. Luckily, both my girls have learned to live within the system and are doing their best. For me, spiritual development has involved making a personal commitment to become a better person and working collaboratively with other people to create a better world, because that is what I genuinely want, not because I fear hell or jail. It's a lifelong endeavor that requires being aware of your actions, thoughts, and feelings, and working to change yourself to meet this goal. I do believe that nowadays more people are making this commitment than in the past."

"Easy to think this way when you live in Oasis. I wonder what you would think if you lived in East," responded James ironically.

"I am no Pollyanna, James, but I must admit that I expected that the disasters would help more people see that any other option would lead to our extinction as a species. What you told us may drive some people to pessimism, but I am determined never to give up and to do my best."

"I admire you, Clara. And I agree. We should be able to thrive in our reality and do our best. Believe it or not, this is my credo too, although my life has taken a different route than yours. See you around."

———————————◆◆◆◆◆◆———————————

The next day Callahan met Ralph, the Oasis banker, who had a hard time recognizing him and, as a result, used all the verification methods in the book to validate his identity. But once convinced, he became friendly and provided invaluable information about Oasis. Among other things, he confirmed that Oasis now legally owned the seven lots previously in Callahan's possession. He added that they'd only succeeded in selling one of them, saying that the owner would be ready to move in within the month. Callahan knew that he had not been entirely fair to the residents. Fighting with them would just backfire. Consequently, he stated that he understood their position and asked if he might receive one of the lots back so he can build a home and settle in Oasis. Ralph promised to raise the question at the next scheduled community meeting, that coming Friday.

After Ralph closed the bank for the day, he gave Callahan and Jacob the grand tour of Oasis. He proudly showed them the community center, the factory, and the home under construction. None of the residents who happened to cross Callahan's path recognized him immediately. He decided to remain anonymous until the community meeting.

Jacob was eager to see Faithfield University, so James drove him over the next day. Jacob loved the small town and the university's flexible schedule, which allowed him to register in the middle of the semester. His counselor, a professor in the Community Building and Design Department, suggested a program that pleased Jacob and accepted the credits Jacob had earned at his former college. He also mentioned work opportunities on projects conducted by the department. Hearing who Jacob's father was, the counselor hinted that they might find an opportunity to utilize his expertise as well.

Jacob wanted to start his new life right away, so he and his father finalized the registration and found a room for him in the student and staff residence with another student who had arrived that same day. James Callahan left his son with some money and returned to Oasis by himself.

CHAPTER 14

EAST IN DISARRAY

Oliphant, who had moved his family away from the Hub following Sarah's escape, celebrated Thanksgiving Day with his family members living in the vicinity of Washington, DC. When he heard about the first attack, which had caused minimal damage, he was relieved. *If that's all Hickman can come up with, I have nothing to worry about,* he thought, rubbing his hands together. He was shocked when he heard about the missile attacks and the thunderous explosions that led to wildfires. Racing ambulances appeared later on in the day on his communications screen. Like all his wealthy OD friends, he had properties in other countries run by his counterparts, hiding behind various labels. Although they did not foresee any danger to the OD regime coming anytime soon, they had plan B just in case. Each OD family had at least one airplane to carry them to safety, and highly paid loyal pilots and mechanics who could execute plan B at any moment. *It is time for plan B,* Oliphant recognized in disbelief. *This is the end,* he thought, grasping the magnitude of the damage before anybody else had. Soon after, his luxurious plane disappeared in the blue sky, heading south, before anybody had a chance to locate him.

For most of Oliphant's supporters who lived away from the Hub, it was time for plan B as well. Still traumatized by the event, they knew very well that their maltreated employees, who were destined to stay behind, would reveal the identities of the OD left behind to the revenge-seeking public in no time. The Hub survivors who had not been seriously injured had to choose between running away and caring for hospitalized loved ones. Many opted for the former, executing plan B, and paying loyal servants to tend the wounded. Nobody cared about burying the dead. The fleeing OD members took with them some of the most loyal mercenaries and servants. Those who were left behind disappeared into the civilian population.

Oliphant's radar spotted multiple airplanes in the air, most going south, but some heading east to Europe. He knew the plans of his supporters but kept his escape route secret, making sure that his hiding place was far from that of any other member. He prepared new identities for himself and his family so that nobody would connect him with the disaster. Otherwise, the followers who blamed him for the disaster would go after him as well.

He was still receiving information about the damage and casualties when he was on his way south. Oliphant remembered that the few experts who knew about the magnitude of the weapons store located at the Hub had ensured him time and again that they had buried the arsenal deep enough so that in the unlikely event their enemies revealed the secret location of the Hub, their missiles would not be able to penetrate the fortified structure that contained the weaponry. How could they have been so wrong? Acknowledging that his leadership had been a failure, Oliphant was dejected but had no remorse.

The damage was enormous. In addition to OD members, many citizens had been killed or injured, and the communities neighboring the Hub were severely damaged. Many survivors who had relatives in Central started making plans to cross over. Among them were Nina and Chloe Solano, Daphne's mother and younger sister, who'd heard about the wedding and knew they would be welcome in Oasis.

East was in disarray. The army was now in control. General Claudio Serafino, chairman of the Joint Chiefs of Staff, instructed his subordinates to maintain order and help with the basic humanitarian needs of the demolished communities. Serafino had not liked Felix Atwell. He had always thought that Gunderson was fitter for the president role than Atwell. Therefore, although suspecting, like others, that Gunderson was the one responsible for Atwell's assassination, Serafino believed that under the current circumstances, he would be the best person to control the mayhem.

Norris Gunderson heard about the missile attack in the prison's cafeteria, where the guards allowed the prisoners to watch the government-controlled news. He was shocked by Oliphant's miscalculation. Although he was an opportunist who did not care for the OD and detested their faux haughtiness, he'd known how to play his cards right to climb in political rank. So, he did not mind seeing the OD evacuating, but he was worried about the implications for him. He hoped that with the OD gone, it would be easier for him to blame the OD for Atwell's assassination. But he needed an ally.

When his guard announced General Serafino's visit, Gunderson was cautiously optimistic. He was led to a closed investigation room. The guard mentioned the general's wish to talk with him privately. The guard left, and the general entered, dressed in shiny, carefully ironed uniform that stood in sharp contrast to the barren grayish room. Gunderson just nodded and waited in anticipation.

"Good morning, Norris. I ordered the guards to allow you to watch the news so I could get right to business. We need a strong interim leader for the country until we can declare an elections date. The Senate majority leader who was sworn into office after Atwell's assassination is a known OD ally. He swiftly declared his resignation after the missile attack. So, here is the deal! I will make sure that you are acquitted if you will take control and prepare for the general elections.

"We all served the OD because we had no choice, but we can become heroes now if we play our cards wisely," he added.

"First for the protocol, I was not involved in Atwell's assassination, but I heard some rumors about an OD order to assassinate him, on the morning of the assassination, when I was in New York on a business trip. Nobody really knows who ordered it. All I know is that many Illuminati believed that Oliphant's leadership was disastrous, so they conspired to get rid of him and his loyal people. Please provide some evidence to accompany my acquittal.

"I accept your offer to become interim president. Please find me somebody who can help me write a convincing speech to the people and make sure that my family and I are safe."

"I am glad we have an understanding. As of now, you are a free man. I will give you a ride home. Your home will continue to be protected for your own safety, but you and your family are no longer prisoners, although I suggest that you not leave without appropriate protection. You will be sworn in tomorrow afternoon with your family in attendance. And I will send somebody to help with the speech."

Gunderson's reunion with his family was emotional and joyous, but soon after his homecoming they had to get busy preparing for their new status. Together they watched the news describing the injustice done to Gunderson by the murderous OD, accompanied by a few testimonies from people accusing the OD of the assassination. The news declared Gunderson, the former vice president, as the legitimate president until the upcoming elections.

The following day, the Supreme Court chief justice swore in the new president. Gunderson delivered the prepared speech promising help to the poor and displaced and ensuring free elections as soon as possible. He encouraged people to submit their candidacy for Congress and the presidency.

In spite of the destruction the missile attack had created, people were happy to see the OD gone and the democracy returning. They were relieved that there was somebody in charge and were willing to accept the claim that the OD had ordered Atwell dead. People cheered and celebrated, welcoming the new president.

The news reached Colorado. Hickman called the last surviving legitimate president, Rockwell, to congratulate him. Rockwell made it clear that since it had been six years since his election, four of which he had spent in exile, he no longer considered himself to be the elected president and was not interested in submitting his candidacy for the upcoming elections. He added that he would love to settle in Colorado and suggested that Hickman be cautious when dealing with East, claiming that they had not seen the end of it yet.

On his first day in office, Gunderson received a phone call from Hickman, who expressed his shock about the outcomes of the attack. He conveyed his regret for the loss of innocent life and offered to end the animosity between East and Central and declare the beginning of a new era in the history of the United States. Gunderson understood very well that, like his predecessor, he would have control only of East, but under the circumstances he did not want to have any conflict with Central. He maintained that he had always been against the OD attacks on Central but had had no influence on their decision. He agreed to end the conflict, expressing the hope that the country would be united again one day. Hickman was quick to remind Gunderson that there was no union, not even within East or Central, just coordination among states, adding that he did not expect this to change in the near future.

+ + + ✦ ✦ ✦ + +

The Geek Clique met to discuss the next steps two weeks after the explosion. Sue, the leader of the group, started the discussion, raising the question of the group's role given the new circumstances. Admired for her wisdom and integrity, the beautiful thirty-eight-year-old curly-haired brunette and mother of two was a natural leader who listened carefully, kept the group on track when people were aimlessly ranting, and led the group to conclusions accepted by all.

Smiling at David, she asked him to report about his trip to Central and thanked him in the name of the group for his courage. He told the group about his conversation with Hickman, and when he mentioned that Riva, the contact suggested by Hickman, was no other than MIT professor Lewandowski, the other six people in the room gasped in surprise. Ray, who used to work for him as a student, noted that according to rumors, Lewandowski disappeared after the explosion. Although they hated the idea that one of them was an OD spy, it made no sense to worry about it now.

Then Sue acknowledged the fragility of the political situation and suggested that since no one in the group was a politician, the group could use its experience with sustainable living to help people displaced by the missile attack and those who used to work in the OD factories and on the farms and were now in limbo. David agreed but argued that they needed to coordinate with the political arm, because eventually the government would decide how to deal with the OD properties and organize the relief projects.

Amalia, Sue's younger sister, intervened, saying that although it

143

is very noble to help those who suffer, the group could do very little about it and needed to make sure that the country had a democracy that works. "As Gunderson and Serafino said," she reminded them, "we need to rethink the party system and find qualified candidates who will honestly serve the people, not themselves." Three people nodded in agreement.

"I nominate you, Amalia," said David jokingly. "I am just a mechanical engineer and systems designer, not a politician. I know how to work with politicians but will never become one."

"I accept the nomination," responded Amalia, looking rather earnest. "I am a business analyst, not a professional politician either, but I have always been interested in politics. I am a member of a group of progressive politicians who think about these issues and attempt to create a better version of the party."

"I am not a politician like the rest of us, and that's why I suggested assisting with sustainable living," said Sue. "But if Amalia wants to run for our legislature, she already has our six votes. My eyes have always looked toward the sky, wondering how we humans could live on other planets. Politics has always seemed to me not just corrupt but also nonsensical. Seriously, please explain to me why we need parties. Why can't good, wise people run as independent candidates without a party, donors, and all the hoopla? Interested smart people can get together and reach consensus without being subjected to a limiting ideology or party platform. Our communications systems can provide means for candidates to explain their positions and communicate with potential voters. The people could vote for the most convincing ones and later judge them by their accomplishments. I am convinced that those elected would work more collaboratively to solve problems, rather than trying to defeat the other party."

"Hmm," responded a contemplative Amalia. "That is an interesting proposition. When you are used to a particular system, you stop wondering how things can be done differently, until something breaks down and you need to fix it. Well, the political system is broken and needs to be fixed. It seems that parties help one organize. I mean, it's arduous for an individual to coordinate a campaign, and consequently good potential candidates may refrain from running."

"Sue is right," contributed Jenny. "We are capable of creating virtual town halls and debates on the public communication system. It should not cost a lot and would enable citizens to participate more actively in the political realm. After all, you can contribute a great idea or a solution to a problem even if you do not run for office. We need to try it."

"I have no clue how you bring it about, but if we are going to be experimenting with a new political system, we should start small. Is it possible to try it with the Massachusetts government?" asked David.

"I will take this suggestion to my group and report back. It won't be easy, because we have a party based-state legislature. And I cannot conceive of an easy way to change it overnight. We can encourage more people to run independently and see how they fare in the elections compared to candidates affiliated with a party. Our group may need to seek some advice from a communications and electronics expert. I hope that our communicator Jenny and our electronic engineer Ray will help. The country's mood is pliable now. We need to make changes before it turns rigid again. We have no time to waste." Amalia's voice was soft but determined.

"I see that most of us are determined to pursue the political route, but I think that the rest of us who would rather work on development should create a subgroup that does just that," concluded Sue.

"By the way, does anybody know what happened to Callahan?" asked David, looking at Sue. "He is your uncle."

"I spoke with my mother in Oasis yesterday, and she told me that Callahan showed up and is interested in settling there. I am not sure about the details of his escape from East and being kidnapped by the Chinese to design communities in California, but it sounds like a thriller to me. Anyway, we sure can contact him for advice, or even invite him to visit us. As a matter of fact, I have not seen my Mom for a long time and would like to go over with the kids, now that it is finally safe. So, I will be able to extend an invitation in person."

Amalia raised the question among her group, and people agreed that in addition to reforming the existing parties, it would be great if people ran as independents and introduced new ideas that would force the parties to rethink their platforms periodically and keep them on their toes. The governor appointed Amalia's group to the team that was preparing for the upcoming elections and promised Massachusetts's citizens that their state would be the first to conduct democratic elections after the fall of the OD. Knowing that all the Central and Western states were governed primarily by their state governments and were integrated loosely by some coordinating boards, the governor argued that it would take a long time to reach an agreement about the structure of the future federal government. He said that each state should reorganize first.

Reforming the existing parties was a harder task than the group had imagined, although the funding for electing colluding politicians had dwindled after the escape of the OD, and the public was ready to punish anybody who showed even a minor degree of sympathy toward the rich and famous. But there was no law against running independently. The networks, noticing the public's thirst for new voices, provided the platform for these candidates to present their ideas and communicate with potential voters.

Amalia was one of thirty candidates running as independent for state congress.

CHAPTER 15

CALLAHAN'S PLIGHT

Callahan had planned to avoid introducing himself to Oasis residents before the community meeting, but fate had it differently. A day before the meeting, he found himself face-to-face with Vanessa, who recognized him immediately and looked horrified.

"James, what are you doing here?"

"Hello, Vanessa. I am happy to see you and was hoping for a more welcoming response. I have been through a lot since we last met, and I would like to settle and find a home here. I am now divorced, but my son is with me. I have just registered him at Faithfield University."

"I am not glad to see you, James. I put the past behind me and created a new life for myself. I have been very peaceful, but now here you are, upsetting my life again."

"The last thing I want to do is to upset you. Can we talk before you jump to conclusions?"

"Okay, you can come with me to my house, but make it short." As they entered Vanessa's home, she asked, "Does Clara know you are here?"

"Yes, she invited Jacob and me for dinner two days ago when we arrived. She was not too happy to see me either."

"So, what makes you want to live here?"

"Everything I've heard about the life in Oasis. The more I see, the more I am convinced that it is the only community that has exceeded my dreams as far as social life goes. To be honest, Vanessa, I also wanted to meet you."

"Forget it, James. I am no longer in this business, and I hate to have a constant reminder of the past."

"You underestimate yourself, Vanessa. I have never treated you like a business, not even when I paid for your services. You have always been a person I could trust. I think the same was true for most of your other clients. You were not the youngest, prettiest, or sexiest woman in the club by any means, but you were the one who would not run to your rival and betray your clients' secrets every time one of them said something he should not have when he was too drunk to think clearly. Like everybody else, you did what you had to do to survive. You would not be here if you had been not there. You would never have had the funds. I cannot tell you how many times I did things I'd rather not have done just to save my neck."

After a moment of silence, she responded, "James, I did not expect you to say this, and I really appreciate it, but I cannot help but remember what I had to go through to earn money. Every time I have contact with somebody from my past is a painful reminder. I wish you had not returned to Oasis."

"Look, Vanessa," he continued, noticing the sudden quiet, "I am not a psychologist, but I learned from my experience that running away from memories, problems, shame, you name it, just makes the mater worse. You should let it all out, face your past, and let it go. You have to accept yourself for who you are. If you are worried that I will talk about it, don't. I am not proud of it either."

"Thank you, but I am not ready to have you or anybody else in my life. I am happy with my life the way it is."

"Think about it, Vanessa. And please don't vote against me tomorrow. Thank you for inviting me in."

The usual group of women, along with Steve, who accompanied Daphne, met in Clara's living room. Stanly was not feeling well. Clara said she needed to journey with the circle and, in place of Stanly's live drumming, would use a recording of shamanic drumming. Everybody in the room looked distracted and worried and seemed to expect the session to resolve all their problems. Clara felt the tension in the room and said that she would lead the group in grounding and relaxation before the journey. She suggested that they focus on one issue and not attempt to solve everything at once.

Following the grounding, she darkened the room and started the recording.

Clara asked about James Callahan. She knew about her sister's feelings toward him and, to a degree, shared those sentiments. However, she both appreciated the way he took care of his son and acknowledged his many talents. She received a message that she should support Callahan since the community needed Callahan as much as he needed the community.

After the callback, Clara asked if anybody wanted to share, but most declined. Steve Grisham mentioned that he had asked for medical advice. He did see the mushroom, but no miracle cure resulted from his journey, only some ideas that he planned to follow through on. Clara nodded, saying that she was not surprised. "Some changes are gradual. The guides are with us even when we do not journey. We need to keep our mind and heart open and listen."

Noticing the somber mood of the participants, who seemed to be dealing with painful personal issues, Clara said, "I have been wanting to teach you a practice to release energy connected to painful past events called recapitulation. I learned it in a workshop of Toltec wisdom years ago and also read about it. I had intended to dedicate a full meeting to it, but I have a feeling that at least some of you can use it right now. So, I've decided to give you the short version of it. Are you willing to stay for a little longer?"

Steve apologized, mentioning that he needed to get to work, but Vanessa, Daphne, Liz, and Freda stayed, waiting with anticipation.

"The purpose of the technique is to heal yourself by restoring energy lost amid traumatic, painful, or shameful events in the past. You see, as long as we do not release the emotional charge of those events, we either suffer thinking about them or invest a lot of energy into keeping them repressed. The technique calls for reliving those events and then releasing the emotional charge by breathing in your energy, the energy you lost because it became attached to the events, and breathing out the energy that is not yours, that is, all the gunk in your soul."

"Are we going to forget our painful past?"

"No, Vanessa, we are going to remember the past, but without the emotional charge. In addition to restoring your energy, it might help you to see the past more clearly and have a deeper understanding of the events. You may see the past differently as well."

"As a social worker, I have used many psychological techniques to deal with my patients' traumas. Are you suggesting that those are invalid?"

"No, Freda, shamanic techniques do not validate or invalidate any other technique. Use what you find to be helpful, and always use your judgment. We are the ones who are responsible for our lives, not the spiritual world. We may ask for and receive help, but we are in the driver's seat. Do you have any more questions?"

Noticing the silence, Clara continued. "Okay, so these are the steps for the procedure. First, you make a list of all the issues you want to release. I suggest that you do this at home. For now, pick only one issue, preferably not the most traumatic or most difficult one.

"Second, set an intent for where you want the energy you gain as a result of the process to go. In other words, visualize how your life will look and what you will be able to accomplish once the issue is resolved.

"Now comes the tough part. Start living the event or events that are related to the issue. Play it in your mind like a video, including as many details as you can remember. As you are doing it, you are to do the breathing work. When you inhale, turn your head from your right shoulder to your left. In so doing, you are reclaiming your energy, the energy that is tied to the painful event and holds you back. When you exhale, move your head from left to right. This expels the energy that does not belong to you and releases your attachment to the event. Feel free to make any sound you like when you exhale. You are kicking the darkness out of your soul."

Vanessa was horrified. The last thing she wanted to do was to relive her past. Painfully she continued to listen.

"Repeat these steps as long as you replay the event and as long as you feel that you need to regain or release more energy, or until you feel no emotional attachment to the issue at all. At the end of the session, you may finish with three quick exhalations. A complete healing may require more than one session, and you may come back to work on the same issue at a different time. Feel free to contact me anytime during or after the session if you have questions. I will do my best to help. So, think about an issue, preferably a simple one, create an intention, start reliving the event, do the breathing work, and at the end, try to feel and enjoy the newly acquired energy."

Clara looked at the briskly moving heads, and heard the loud exhalations expressing at times anger, pain, and disgust. She was pleased to learn that the group got it. When they all finished working on their problem, they seemed to be eager to leave and do more work at home. They thanked Clara and walked out.

Vanessa was exhausted. She had not slept last night, looking forward to Clara's drumming circle. There were so many questions she wanted to ask before the community meeting took place in the evening. Deep down inside, she knew that James was right and she needed to come to terms with her past. Meeting him now was a necessary part of the process. She needed help without having to disclose her past. Clara, whose wisdom and integrity she admired and envied, was the only one who could help her, through journeying.

Before journeying, Vanessa had asked for insight into James Callahan's reappearance in her life. As the drumming started, she felt deeply that James's arrival was to her advantage, since it would help her free herself from the past, regardless of what their future relationship would look like. Her guide suggested that she should support his acceptance into the community and most importantly tell him the secret she had been hiding.

As she walked home, she was amazed at the timing of Clara's new teaching of recapitulation, knowing that she needed to create a very long list and work on those issues. She could not run away from the past anymore and needed some quiet time to grapple with it. Now, she regretted that she had not done it years ago, before James reappeared in her life.

But time has its way of playing games with us. When we most need time for reflection and recuperation, life gushes toward us mercilessly, asking us to make fast critical decisions, cope, and prevail. As soon as Vanessa got home, her telephone rang.

Vanessa felt a chill when she answered the phone. A raspy female voice asked for Vanessa Edwards, and Vanessa confirmed that she was that person.

"Hello, Vanessa. My name is Edith Spears. I am the adoptive mother of your son. We named him Morris. He is a wonderful ten-year-old boy. I wish I didn't need to contact you. I love him so much. My late husband and I did everything we could to see him grow to be a happy child. My husband died two years ago in the big flood, and I have worked hard to keep us afloat."

The woman started sobbing. Vanessa was frozen. *Oh my God, I am not ready to deal with this now.*

"Thank you for taking care of him," responded Vanessa, sitting down on the sofa, almost fainting. "I am sure you are a great mother to him, much better than I could have ever been. Why are you telling me this now?"

"Last week I was diagnosed with a terminal disease. I am bedridden and am not sure how long I have. I lost my family and know nobody who will take care of Morris. I wish I could have contacted you earlier. A social worker helped me, and she has just located you. Please come to see us. I hope that now you may be able to take care of your son. You see, the Faithville orphanage is horrible. Your son needs you now." She continued sobbing.

"Does he know that he is adopted?"

"I told him a week before my diagnosis. I felt sick already. He said that deep down inside he'd felt it, because he resembles neither me nor my husband, or anybody in our families. He asked why his mother left him, and I told him that you were not married to his father, worked hard to survive, and did not have the means to raise him. We want to meet you. Can you come to see us tomorrow? Maybe between 4:00 and 5:00 p.m.?"

Vanessa was shivering as she heard herself answering, "Yes, I will be there." She was not ready for meeting her son and could not believe that she agreed. It felt as if a higher power, not she, was in the driver's seat and making the decisions for her. After hanging up with Edith, she called James and told him she needed to see him as soon as possible.

James arrived shortly thereafter. "What is wrong?" he asked, seeing a shaking Vanessa.

"I no longer know what is right and what is wrong. Maybe this is right."

"Can you explain what you just said?"

Following a big sigh, she answered, "Ten years ago I gave birth to a baby boy, our son. I don't understand why I decided to keep the pregnancy. You had already left town, you were married, and I knew there was no way I could raise this child on my own. But I could not make myself go to the doctor. I succeeded in hiding my pregnancy and put the child up for adoption. I told myself that I was not good enough to be a mother and just tried to forget that I had ever given birth to a son. Just before I called you, Morris's adoptive mother called. Her husband died two years ago, and she has just been diagnosed with a terminal disease. She expects me to take over and asked me to visit tomorrow. I agreed."

"Vanessa, I know we had a relationship at that time, but it cannot be my son. My doctor told me that I couldn't have children and that Jacob was a fluke. It must be somebody else's. Besides, how did it happen? I was sure you were taking precautions."

"My doctor told me that I could not have children as well because of some complications, and therefore I was not careful. There was no other man in my life at that time. You are the boy's father. I am not telling you that to make you feel guilty or even responsible. I never thought I'd tell you about it when we met again. This phone call changed everything. What am I going to say to the child if he asks about his father?"

"I have no clue, Vanessa. I only know that I am not ready to be in that spot. Why did you agree to take him back?"

"I betrayed him once; I cannot do it again. As you said, I can no longer run away from my past. For once, I want to do the right thing."

"See you at the meeting tonight."

People started gathering for the evening meeting, chatting and laughing. Just before 8:00 p.m. Charlotte showed up, strutting across the gathering area. All in attendance seemed to look the other way.

Noticing Vanessa, Charlotte approached her with a big artificial smile. "Hi, Vanessa. I would love to move back to Oasis. Can I rent your guest room again? I will pay you more than before."

"Sorry, Charlotte, I need that room now." Vanessa turned her back to Charlotte and moved away.

Charlotte, quite surprised, noticed Rudolph and asked him if there was a room to rent in the community, expressing disappointment after he said that there were none.

Apparently, the rumors about James's return had reached Faithville. Now Charlotte was looking for him. When she spotted James entering, she pretended not to see him. Assuming that Freda, the devoted social worker, would not refuse to listen, Charlotte disclosed that her relationship with the doctor in Blessed Health was over, because his two monsters did not like her. Freda tried to be kind but told her unequivocally that she had better leave.

"Why does everybody hate me?"

"You hurt too many people, and they would rather not see you around here."

Charlotte left Freda and pretended to bump into James unintentionally. She feigned surprise at seeing him there, but it was evident to everybody that somehow she had heard about his return and was attempting to rekindle the flame.

To her greeting, he just answered "I am not interested," and looked the other way. Charlotte could not believe it. It was impossible that he would find Vanessa or Liz, the only available women in Oasis, more attractive than her. But it was getting late, and she had no place to stay in Oasis. Stanly, who wanted to start the meeting, approached her and told her flatly, "We are going to have a members' meeting, and you are not a member, so please leave." She turned around and went back to her car.

Callahan came to the meeting with low expectations. Nobody seemed to be glad to see him. He thought ironically that Vanessa was not the only one who needed to come to terms with the past. He wanted to start over, but every new occurrence brought the past back to life. First, the encounter with Vanessa had introduced another dimension to his life, and then he had run into Charlotte, who represented the time when he was wild and reckless. He had an urge to run away from it all, but given his lack of success finding a job, he knew that he should give Oasis his best shot.

Callahan was relieved when Stanly announced that the first item on the agenda was his request to become a member. Stanly invited him to explain to the members why they should agree and what he could contribute to the community.

Callahan retold an abbreviated version of all his travails since he'd last visited Oasis. He knew that there were rumors about his relationship with the OD and tried to paint a picture of his time in East in the brightest colors he could. He described the juicy details of his escape and kidnap, how he lost his wife in East and found her in California, and how he left with his son, who was currently studying at FSUni. Then he talked about his desire to contribute his experience to the community, emphasizing that although Oasis was the least luxurious of all the communities he'd built, its community life best resembled his vision, and even exceeded his wildest dreams.

"James, we are not foolish," interrupted Rudolph quite sarcastically. You are not going to convince anybody here that you are an idealist. We all know you only cared about getting your money back and making a nice profit."

"You are wrong, Rudolph. Sure, I wanted to recover the money I'd invested and make some profit. Leaving the community center unfinished was the only way to do it after I reduced the price of the homes for most of you. But this place was my dream. I spent hours designing the communities and hired the best of the best. I thought about every aspect to ensure physical survival and foster a sense of community. I was convinced that a cohesive community was the only guarantee of survival. Unfortunately, having it all does not guarantee an integrated community. I lived in a more affluent community where people were divided into two tribes that hated each other. I also heard horror stories about Sanctuary. In hindsight, I think that having to finish the building of the center yourselves was to your advantage. I have not seen any community that uses the community center as extensively as you use yours. You own it. It is your home, and hopefully mine too."

"Are you interested in a job in Sustainit?" asked Donna, contemplating his potential contribution to the company.

"I would sure be glad to have a job close to home."

Stanly started the voting process. Freda, Rudolph, Daphne, and Steve abstained. The rest voted in Callahan's favor.

James could hardly hide his emotions. Teary-eyed, he found that all he could say was, "Thank you, my friends. I cannot find words to describe what your acceptance means to me. I promise you that you will not regret your decision."

"We sure hope so," replied Stanley, tapping James on the shoulder.

Vanessa spent the rest of the evening praying and recapitulating. With dread, she drove to town the next day, hoping to convince Edith to keep Morris for a little longer so that she could prepare herself for the motherhood role. She was trembling when she knocked on the door, yet she was curious to see what her son looked like.

A woman opened the door and shook Vanessa's hand.

"Hello, Vanessa. I am Lisa, the social worker who helped Edith find you. Please come in. They are waiting for you." Vanessa could smell the scent of disease, which filled the air. She followed Lisa, glancing at Morris's belongings, all packed and ready to go. Then she saw him, the child she never thought she would meet. She looked at him and started crying. His resemblance to James was stunning. He was tall for his age, and strong, with the same dark hair and powerful angular jawline as James. She stood there not believing that she had brought this wonderful child into the world.

"I am glad to see you, Morris," she said softly. He looked at her and said nothing.

Edith looked very sick and certainly could no longer take care of him. Vanessa kneeled by the bed, terrified by Edith's appearance of imminent death. "Thank you, Edith. I will do my best," she mumbled. Edith just nodded.

He must hate me for giving him up, thought Vanessa, acknowledging that Morris did not look happy to see her.

Lisa notified her that they were going to move Edith to the hospital, adding that after Vanessa signed some papers, she would be able to take Morris with her. When neither of them made a move, Lisa tried to break the ice.

"Morris, this is your mom. She could not take care of you when you were born, but now she can. She has a charming home in Oasis, and I am sure you will have a good life there. It may take some time, but you will learn to love each other."

"Mommy, please stay with me," he said, running to Edith and hugging her.

"Remember that even in heaven I will always look after you.

I love you, Morris. Be good to your mom." Very feebly she added, "Vanessa, I am sure you will be a great mother."

Lisa helped Vanessa move Morris's belongings to the car. Morris clung to his mother, refusing to move.

"Come, Morris. We will visit your mom next weekend, I promise you. Now she must be treated in the hospital and get some rest," said Vanessa.

"Goodbye, Son. May God always protect you."

Vanessa and Morris left. They drove home in silence. Vanessa's clumsy attempts to engage Morris in small talk were met with hostile silence. She noticed that Morris was trying to conceal his weeping. Wondering if she had done the right thing bringing him with her, she knew deep down inside that any other response would have been wrong.

"Okay, Morris, we are home," she said, trying to sound cheerful. The garage door closed behind them. Please help me carry your belongings to your room. I did not know you would come back with me today, so I did not prepare my guest room for you." Once they were in the guest room, she said to him, "Please take a look at the room and let me know if you want to make any changes. And start unpacking."

Morris shifted the desk toward the window and hung some posters. In no time, the room started looking like the room of a ten-year-old boy.

Vanessa knew she needed some help, and fast. A few names crossed her mind. First, she thought about James, but she was acutely aware that she had better not call him now. She thought she would need a psychologist. Freda the social worker was the next best thing. She decided to start with Laura, the school coordinator.

"Morris, I am going to call your new school coordinator. I need to let her know that she will have a new student tomorrow!"

"I hate school!"

"You will love this one. It has just the children of the community."

"What are you going to tell her about me?"

"The truth."

Vanessa mused that the truth might not be as hard to tell as answering the expected question about the identity of the father would be.

She picked up the phone and called Laura, briefly telling her the story.

Laura was silent for a moment. Then she told Vanessa that she would gladly have Morris as a new student.

"Bring him to school tomorrow at eight o'clock. Is it okay if I ask Freda to help and conduct an assessment? He must be traumatized. Oh, I think that I will also talk with Liz. Her son Karl is about Morris's age."

"Sure, Laura. Do what you think would help Morris to feel at home here." She hung up and turned to Morris.

"I think I should fix something for dinner. What do you like to eat?"

"I am not hungry."

"Well, then I will just put a few things on the table and you can choose what you wish to eat." She added proudly, "All the fruits and vegetables, fresh, cooked, canned, or pickled, are from my garden."

"I didn't know you had a garden!"

"We all have! And there is also one in the community center where your school is located. I can show it to you after we finish eating."

"Maybe later," he answered, turning his back and running to his room. Vanessa could hear him crying.

The doorbell rang. Callahan entered without waiting to be invited inside.

"Hi, Vanessa. Thanks for your vote yesterday. Want to join me at the center?"

"He is here! In his room."

He heard the child's sobbing and felt a pain in his chest. He had planned to talk Steve into performing a paternity test once Morris came for a checkup, but his gut feeling was that the second child he and Sophie had tried desperately to conceive had been born unbeknown to him.

"Do you want me to leave?"

"It's totally up to you, James. I am staying with Morris tonight. You are welcome to join us for dinner."

Morris stepped in. James looked at his face and froze. It was clear that he would not need a paternity test, and everybody else would at least suspect that he is the father. "Good evening, Morris. Vanessa told me about you, but I did not know that she would bring you here tonight. I am so sorry about your parents."

"Are you my father?"

It took him a minute to answer. "Yes, Son, I am, although I only found out about it yesterday." He rushed to him and gave him a big hug. "I am proud of you and am glad you are here. I will be around a lot."

A knock on the door was followed by Freda stepping in. A quick look around the room and the sight of the three of them explained the situation better than words could. Being a social worker, she was used to tackling awkward situations and had learned to show no emotion.

"Good evening. Laura told me that we have a new student in school. I came to see if you need any help."

Vanessa looked confused and could not figure how to answer the question. James thanked Freda and said that there was not much to do this evening, but it would be helpful if she could help Morris settle in at school. She nodded and encouraged Morris to seek her out should he have a problem.

"I assume that you are his father," she said harshly.

"Freda, please don't judge me. I just found out yesterday that I have another son."

"I am not judging. You look great as a father."

Looking at Vanessa, she could not avoid a deep sigh. "Please come to see me. I am here to help.

"See you tomorrow," she said. Then she left.

"Do I have a brother or a sister?" asked Morris, addressing James.

"Yes, Morris, you have a half-brother. He and I arrived at Oasis just a few days ago. He registered at Faithville University and is so happy there that he has no time for his father. You see, I was married and already had a son when I met your mother. I liked your mother very much, but when I finished my business here, I returned to my family on the East Coast. This was before I found out that she was pregnant with you. That is why she decided to put you for adoption. She wanted to make sure you had a good father and mother."

"Did your wife come with you too?"

"No. She is no longer my wife. She married another man and is pregnant with his child. It's getting late, and we are all tired. If you need me, try to fetch me in my motor home, the one parked by the community center. Some guy who is building a home here has changed his mind and now wants to sell. I am going to meet him tomorrow, and if everything works well, I will have a home that you would enjoy visiting."

Callahan left, leaving Vanessa was alone with her son.

CHAPTER 16

VANESSA

After James left, Vanessa stood dejected, feeling like a complete failure. The guilt for putting her child up for adoption, hidden in the corner of her subconscious for ten years, surfaced with a vengeance. Not only could she not be a decent mother to her son when he was born, but also now that she had the means, she was incapacitated as a mother. *James had taken no time to relate to a child he was previously unaware of, but I do not know how to communicate with the son I gave birth to,* she thought. And she loathed the name Morris. It felt that everything was wrong, and she had no clue how to fix it. She was lost in her thoughts, not noticing that Morris was standing behind her.

Hearing him coughing, she turned her head and saw him.

"Time to sleep, Morris. It has been a tough day for both of us. I may not be the best mother, but I will do my best to help you grow."

The following day she prepared some breakfast and followed her son to school. At school, they met Laura, who ensured Vanessa that she had prepared the children for the arrival of the new student, saying that the class was looking forward to meeting him. Vanessa listened as Laura asked Morris about the curriculum in his previous school. Then Laura administered some tests. Morris looked concerned, but Laura reassured him and Vanessa that she was very impressed and he would be an appropriate addition to the class of Karl and Denise, who were one year older than he, and eight-year-old Deena.

"I am sure he will love his new school. Don't worry, you can leave now," she told Vanessa. The two were accompanying Morris to his study group, which was heading out to the garden.

After dropping Morris off at school, Vanessa asked for a day off. She realized that her emergency provisions would suffice for one person but hardly for two, and certainly not for possible three. Many rumors were circling about the imminent severe windstorm. Being a zealous follower of the emergency supply list, Vanessa was anxious to get the necessary provisions at once. Her only concern was whether her truck was large enough to carry all she needed and if she would have sufficient funds. She assumed she would be able to ask James to share expenses. She drove to town thinking about the new clothes she had planned to buy for Morris after noticing how little he'd brought with him.

Oasis residents, including the shop owner, were used to purchasing canned and boxed food and other necessities from three wholesalers in Faithfield. Vanessa knew them quite well and planned to visit all three, as each had some products she liked that the others did not. She started with George's Supplies, which was located the farthest from Oasis.

She presented the seller with a list and was stunned to hear that he was leaving town and trying to sell everything he could not take with him. He dodged her repeated questions about the reason for his sudden move and finally uttered in an unconvincing manner that he was leaving for family and personal reasons. He sold Vanessa everything he had left at a good price, and she proceeded to the second wholesaler, Steve's Inventory.

From a distance, she could see the Liquidation Sale sign. She felt panicky and got what she could. Again, her attempts to understand what was going on were met with hollow answers. She expected a déjà vu experience at Stock Your Pantry, and indeed it did happen again—unintelligible mumbling by way of an explanation. After buying everything she could, she checked her list. What she had bought would do for now, but how about the future? She decided that she must notify Oasis residents at once!

Before leaving town, she stopped at a warehouse where she used to buy clothes for a good price. A sigh of relief. The store was open, and she was able to find some pants, some shirts, some boots, and a coat for Morris. She started a conversation with the cashier about the wholesalers leaving town. He shrugged and said that everybody was talking about the coming disaster, saying that people should keep what they have and avoid selling.

Then she visited the town supermarket and bought a few things, but she felt a chill looking at the half-empty shelves. When she approached the grocery shop at the north end of town, she heard what sounded to her like rifle shots, and drove home as fast as she could.

She entered the Oasis store and got what she needed. Trembling, she approached the counter. Fred popped out from the storage area.

"Hi, Vanessa, what is wrong? You look terrible!"

"I have just come from Faithville. I went there to restock my pantry, as I need to provide for Morris. Fred, everyone there is leaving town! What are we going to do?"

"Who is leaving town?"

"All our providers! George's Supplies, Steve's Inventory, Stock Your Pantry—they are all selling out and leaving town. I could not get everything on my list. The southern grocery is half empty, and I heard shootings coming from the north grocery's direction, so I did not check it out."

Fred knew that Vanessa would not make up a story like this. He promised her that he would talk with Stanly. She left. To be sure, he decided to check out her story. After all, George and Steve were business buddies and close friends. George told him that he'd sold everything to Vanessa and was already on his way north, saying that nobody was selling and everybody is hoarding. Steve from Steve's Supplies was packing to get ready to leave tomorrow. Fred called Stanley, who decided to summon the entire community for a meeting that evening.

Vanessa prepared a nice dinner and asked James to join her and Morris. When Morris returned from school, she felt somewhat less inhibited and asked him about his day.

"I like this school; it's not like my former school. The kids are friendly, and so are the teachers. I already made a new friend—Karl. I love the work in the garden."

"You can help me in my garden as well if you wish," she said, thinking they might bond working together in the greenhouse. "I took a day off to buy you a few clothes. I have noticed that you are outgrowing what you brought. Please try them on. I hope they fit."

The clothes and boots were a little too big, but they were very nice, and Morris knew they would fit him in a few months. He smiled at Vanessa. She found herself giving him a warm hug.

"I am glad you like your school and your new clothes. I promise you that I will do my best to make your life as happy as I can and keep you safe."

"Thanks, Mom!"

Vanessa smiled. The word *Mom* filled her heart with a tender happiness she had never known before. Her heart was exploding. *Mom*; what a beautiful word.

James entered without knocking.

"Vanessa, do you know why we are having a meeting tonight?"

"Unfortunately I do. I brought up the worrisome news about the closing of all three wholesale stores in Faithville. We will have to decide what to do about it. Let's have a quick dinner before we leave."

"Am I going too?" Morris's voice was quite surprised.

"Sure, Morris. All the kids will be there. They are part of the community and listen to the discussions. That is how you learn. When you reach the age of eighteen, you will be able to vote as well."

"I like the idea of being part of the community and can't wait to see my new friends."

The three of them arrived at the center and sat together, Morris between James and Vanessa, trying to ignore the curious looks sent in their direction. They felt the anxious anticipation of those who could not fathom what had caused this emergency meeting.

Stanly recounted Vanessa's story briefly, and then turned to Rudolph, asking him about the validity of the disaster rumors.

"I heard the rumors. There are reasons to be worried but certainly not to panic. We have been through this before, and the usual precautions, of well-stocked pantries and well-maintained weather shields and air filters, should suffice. There are menacing weather patterns on the horizon. I expect strong, cold north winds and a colder than ever winter. However, much more worrisome is the news of a nuclear explosion in the Middle East, probably Iran.

The information is sparse, so we are not sure if it was an accident or an act of war. It has caused major earthquakes in the area that might have a ripple effect on the other side of the globe, possibly California. I do not expect to see any signs of it around here, but I am following the heartbeat of Mother Earth. Air contamination is a more serious possibility, and we should prepare for it in case we are affected. I have notified Donna and Mark."

"James, why don't you tell them about your team?" asked Donna. James stood up, noticing an admiring look from his son and Vanessa.

"As you know, I joined Sustainit this morning. My first assignment was to head a team that is looking into local air-filtration systems. I am still learning but am already impressed by the advances made by Sustainit teams since I was last involved with Oasis. I have succeeded in getting a hold of some patented Chinese systems that were used in Korea but brought to California as a defense against potential OD attack. My teammates and I have some ideas about putting the components together in a way that controls the outdoor air around our community. In the meantime, we are double-checking all the systems to make sure that people are safe, which you are as long as you do not leave home."

"What are we going to do about the food shortage?" asked Freda. "We had been through climate-related disasters before but not the disappearance of suppliers." More angry comments ensued. Fred tried calming the people's agitation, boasting that his large stock would suffice for about six months. But this news only made the people more anxious.

"What will happen after six months?" shouted many. Fred did not have a clear answer.

Stanly attempted to move the conversation in a different direction. "Being angry is not going to solve any of our problems. We survived many hardships because we stuck together, kept calm, and solved problems. Does anyone have any suggestions?"

Vanessa rose up, and everybody quieted down at once. "The only way to survive is to produce more in the community. We started by having personal greenhouses and having a farmer living among us, and then we added the community greenhouse. It seems that this is not enough. We need to produce more, both for our needs and for exchanging food for items we cannot produce here. We still have six lots that belong to the community. We can use those to raise more animals and grow more food. We need to elect a committee that will plan out how to produce what we need. Sustainit can design protected greenhouses and barns. Thanks to our robotic systems, it will not require a lot of extra work, but we will have to work more within Oasis and less outside."

"These lots were designated as places for taking care of our children or other relatives," said Clara.

"More people require more food, Clara. I reflected on possible outcomes of the upcoming disasters. There are going to be many refugees, and we will want to help at least our families and friends. We can live less comfortably and take in more people, but we will need more food."

Stanly asked the members to vote on Vanessa's proposal. In the absence of other ideas, the community voted for it unanimously. Frustrated to have to produce more necessities in Oasis than they already were producing, residents acknowledged that there was no other way.

"We need a planning committee. James, you designed our community and others like it. Are you willing to chair the committee?"

"Yes. I participated in similar projects for the Chinese in California and kept copies of some of our inventions and designs. We can adapt them to our needs."

"Any more nominations?" asked Stanly.

"Liz," shouted Ralph, the banker.

"I will serve on the committee, but I don't want to chair it. I second James's nomination."

"Any objections?" asked Stanly. "None. So, James, you are the chair, joined by Liz, our dedicated farmer, and Fred, our resourceful shopkeeper. Who else?"

James said, "I would like to have a representative of Sustainit. Vanessa is a good candidate because she is also the community treasurer, but it can be whomever Mark and Donna nominate. I also want Dr. Grisham to participate. I know that he studied the nutritional quality and yields of many crops, and also medicinal plants."

People smiled when he mentioned Vanessa.

"James, you forgot that as of this morning you are on our payroll as well, but I agree that Vanessa should be on the board," responded Mark. Donna just nodded.

"Steve, will you join my team?" asked James, remembering that he was one of the four who had abstained during the vote to accept him as a member."

"Yes, I will, and thank you for inviting me. I have developed new methods to preserve foods in various ways, powder form included. And Daphne, in the privacy of our kitchen, is developing ways to make sure that the products are tasty, not merely nutritious. This will be crucial when we produce more food and try to sell it outside our community, or store it here to be used in the event of inclement weather."

"I think we have all the right people in the right places," said Stanley, smiling. "Anything else?"

"Yes, Stanly," James responded. "I wanted to announce that Uri Valero, whose under-construction home is almost ready to move into, offered to sell it to me, because he's decided to stay in Faithville. We are still negotiating the details, but I hope to own a home in Oasis soon. Thank you for allowing me to use one of the unsold lots for building my home on. I hope it will not be necessary and that we will be able to use all six unbuilt lots for shared goals. I am glad that my confiscated lots are going to be used for a good purpose. I honestly am."

"I ask the members of the planning committee to stay for an initial discussion after the adjourning of this emergency meeting."

Vanessa felt that her renewed hopes of having a man in her life and a father to Morris had dissipated, but being used to suppressing her feelings, she hid her disappointment. After a short meeting of the planning committee, James accompanied her and Morris home. Before he bade them good night, and after kissing her on her forehead, he said softly, "I am not going to move in with you at this point, but I will always be here for Morris and you."

CHAPTER 17

SUE

Sue could not fathom how her life had fallen apart during the previous week. She had returned from the Geek Clique meeting with many plans for future activities at work, at home, and in the community and could not wait to share them with Josh, her husband. Josh had been busy with his work in geological and geothermal studies and hadn't joined the group. Still, he had always been curious about the group's activities because he knew all the participants very well.

Surprisingly, Josh was not home when Sue returned from the meeting, and her two teenage boys had not heard from him either. She started worrying when he did not respond to her various attempts to communicate with him, but she tried to hide her feelings from the kids, busying herself with supper preparations. She breathed a sigh of relief when she heard the sound of Josh's footsteps at the door.

"Hello there. Have you been in the stratosphere? Why didn't you answer my messages?"

"Because I needed to talk with you in person."

Sue, accompanied by the two boys, who had come over to greet their father, looked at him in astonishment.

"Well, you are all here, so I will get to the point without any introduction. Hmm, what I am trying to say is that I am going to leave. I will always take care of you, but I am moving in with a woman I have known for quite some time. We finally decided to get together. I am going to pack the essentials tonight, and we will talk about the details of the separation later."

Neither Sue nor the boys said a word. Sue felt that a massive stone had settled in her heart. She could hardly breathe. Being a strong and fiercely proud woman, she calmly invited the boys to eat supper. Nobody had the appetite to eat much. The boys grabbed something and hurried to their rooms. Sue cleaned up the kitchen and then retreated to her little study. Only when she heard the door closing behind Josh did she allow the tears to fall profusely onto her cheeks.

Two days later, she was summoned by her boss, the head of the Astro Studies Department, who told her that because of budget cuts and a reduced interest in astro studies, the department was going to cut three positions, hers included, and this semester would be her last. Her financial situation looked very grim. They still had a mortgage on the home, and without a job, she could not stay at home and manage to make the payments. Josh offered a generous amount of money for her and the boys' share of the home. She felt that she had no choice but to accept the offer, in spite of the disgust she felt when she found out that some of the money would be paid by Lucy, Josh's new flame.

Sue knew that her chances of securing another job in the Northeast were zilch and that if she rented a place in the area, she would use up all her savings quickly. Since Danny would complete middle school and Amos would finish grade school by the end of the semester, in two weeks, she decided not to make any move until then, but what next? She picked up the phone.

"Mom?!"

Clara's face appeared on the screen. Her voice sounded worried. "Sue, darling, is everything okay? You never call in the morning hours."

"Nothing is okay, Mom. Josh left me for another woman and offered some money if the kids and I leave. I lost my job, so I cannot pay the mortgage anyway ..."

"Take the kids, load as much as you can into your vehicle, and come over at once. If you need to stay longer, such as until the school year is over, don't leave home until you are ready to move. Don't waste your time; start looking for another job. Why don't you start with Faithfield State University? Some Oasis residents work there and can talk to the right people on your behalf. Send me your resume, and I will see what I can do. Be strong and don't worry. Everything will turn out okay."

"Mom, you do not look surprised. Don't tell me you knew it through reading your Akashic records or some other spiritual activity."

Clara chuckled. "No spiritual activity, Sue, just my intuition, or psychic ability if you prefer. I have never trusted Josh, and have never liked him either. He was your husband and the father of my grandsons, so I did not demonstrate how I felt. Given how little I saw him, it was not that hard to do. I don't think he liked your dad or me either. As far as your job is concerned, it will take a long time before humanity renews its interest in colonizing Mars. If the forecast for imminent catastrophic disasters is correct, we will have to think about new ways of living here on Earth. You can refocus your research to meet these challenges."

"You are right about the research. I tried to talk my department head into allowing me to do just that, but he was determined to let me go. And my chances of finding a job in the East are slim. I did not know you did not like Josh, though. Anyway, I will transfer you my resume. I am sure I can get good recommendations from some colleagues if needed."

Unlike Clara, Amalia was shocked to hear the news. She was furious about Josh, stunned that her talented sister was let go, and above all perturbed that Sue was going to leave town for good. Amalia was very close to Sue and consulted her before making any important decision. So, Sue found herself in the unlikely position of consoling her sister and promising her that everything would be just fine.

"You are going to win your seat in the Massachusetts House of Representatives and will be so busy that you will not even have time to think about me. And if you need to talk, I will be on the other end of the line. Thankfully, the communications system has proven itself even during disasters. My boys would like to be in touch with their cousins, and Mom and Dad would love to see more of you as well. So, we will continue to be in touch."

"Sure, Sue, but it is not the same as having you as a neighbor. Mom is also sure I am going to win the seat. I am not so sure, and am working hard to advertise on the Election Network. I have developed many initiatives and want potential voters to be aware of them. The elections are less than a week from today. So much to do and so little time!"

"That's my amazing little sister doing all the right things. I will miss you, Amalia, but I must leave. I hope to be able to find a job at Faithville State University. Mom is already making sure that my resume reaches the right people."

"That's Mom all right! No storm is strong enough to shake her!"

"I wouldn't go that far, but yes, she is strong—and so am I. And believe it or not, so are you, Amalia."

"Okay, Sis, let me know if you need help packing or anything else, and make sure to get your van checked before leaving. I still can't believe this is happening!"

++◆◆◆++

Clara wasted no time. She printed out Sue's resume, left home, and walked around the community center, hoping to catch Steve before he left for work. She noticed his car leaving the garage and waved him to stop. He got out of his car. *"Is Stanly okay?"* he asked. Clara handed him Sue's resume and explained the situation in brief.

"She is exactly what we need! Well, I am sorry about her family situation and her layoff, but their loss is our gain. Don't worry, Clara, I know exactly who I should talk to."

Steve went directly to his dean and showed him the resume.

"Are you telling me that Dr. Susanna Salomon is on her way here? I am familiar with her work. I had a long conversation with her years ago at a conference. Of course, I cannot offer her the salary she received in Boston, but I will do my best. Please let her know that she is welcome here."

"Why don't you do it yourself? I am sure she could use some good news."

With Steve in attendance, the dean picked up the phone.

"Dr. Susanna Salomon? I am Dick Pickering from the Sustainability Department at Faithville State University. I believe we met years ago at a conference in Seattle. I heard that you are coming to Oasis. Dr. Steve Grisham handed me your resume. I didn't have to read it, though, because I am familiar with your work. I would like to extend an invitation to you to join our faculty as a full-time professor. We can discuss the specifics when you arrive in town."

"Thanks, Dick. Please call me Sue. I am overwhelmed. I accept your offer. When can I start?"

"Tomorrow, as far as I am concerned! Let me know when you are ready to begin."

At supper, Sue beamed at her children and informed them that she had just accepted a job in Faithville and that they would be moving in with their grandparents as soon as the school year was over.

Fourteen-year-old Amos looked excited. "I hope they have no school in Oasis."

"I don't want to leave all my friends. I want to stay here and go to middle school with them," lamented twelve-year-old Danny.

"I am sure both of you will love Oasis, and yes, they have a small, charming school there. As you know, I lost my job here. Today, I was offered a position at Faithville State University. So, start thinking about what you want to pack."

Amalia and her children showed up at the door. "Sue, did you hear the news? The city council decided to shorten the school year by two weeks because of the impending disasters. They are talking about a quick rise in the sea level, well above the already high current level, and are very concerned that the seawalls and levees will not hold. I don't think it will reach Prosperity, but it's going to affect many people. The last school day is tomorrow. I must attend an emergency meeting, and Dave is not back from work yet. Can Evie and Saul stay here until Dave picks them up?"

"Of course they can. It will be their last chance to say goodbye. If school is over tomorrow, we had better leave the day after tomorrow, before the forecasted disasters. By the way, I have accepted a job offer from Faithville State University."

Two days later, early in the morning, Sue programmed the autopilot, and then she and the two boys were on their way to Colorado. She took the money Josh had offered for the home and left the keys with Amalia, since Josh did not show up to say goodbye to the kids. The two teenagers had mixed feelings. They were excited about the new adventure, as it had been a long time since they had traveled anywhere, but they grieved over what they had left behind and their father's unfathomable behavior.

Three days after they left, late at night, exhausted, they heard the garage door closing behind them in Oasis. The next thing they heard was the deafening noise of thunder and strong winds. Clara and Stanly happily hugged them, relieved that they had made it before the storm set in. They helped to empty the van, offered some food, and helped them to their rooms, where beds covered with freshly washed bedding were ready for them.

"You are safe now. We have activated our protective screen to defend our home and greenhouse. Rudolph notified the community that he has turned on the shielding blanket."

"The what?!"

"The shielding blanket is one of the latest inventions of Sustainit. It protects us against extreme weather by, among other things, reducing the strength of the winds and diverting excessive rainwater to the nearby reservoir. Your uncle, or ex-uncle, Callahan now works in the company and would be able to explain how it works much better than I can. We activate it only when the forecast calls for dangerous weather conditions. That's why we are relieved to see you here!"

"Mom, East is in a total disarray. States are trying to reorganize after the escape of the OD and the distraction caused by Central's bombing. And they expect a flood due to the rising sea level. People are not ready to cope with another disaster. Do you know if East is going to be affected by the storm? We need to call Amalia at once!"

"I have tried. It seems that communication lines have been severed. I could not reach her. We will try again tomorrow."

"Oh my God! Why do I feel the need to be thankful for Josh's betrayal?" Her sentence was cut off by rolling thunder, which made the boys jump out of bed and run to the living room. Heavy rain and tornado-force winds ensued, and the skies were lit with natural fireworks. Clara reassured the kids, telling them that here in Oasis they were used to these storms and were fully protected. She hoped she was right this time, knowing very well that other places were less lucky.

"I need to inform Dr. Dick Pickering, my future boss, that I arrived safely," said Sue, remembering suddenly that he might be worried.

The phone rang when Sue was jotting down a message. Clara picked up the receiver.

"Clara, it is James. Have Sue and the boys arrived safely?"

"Yes. I have just tucked the boys in bed. I did not realize you cared."

"Come on, Clara! I am sick and tired of these innuendoes. It is not I who left your sister; it was the other way around. And don't forget that you all live in my developments, thanks a great deal to my help. Oh, I want Sue to join our planning committee. Do you think she will be able to join us tomorrow at the 9:00 a.m. teleconference?"

"You don't waste any time, James." Her voice hinted at the admiration she felt for Callahan's creativity and ability to get things done efficiently.

"There is no time to waste, Clara. Our community has grown overnight. Besides Sue and the boys, I have heard from Steve that Daphne's mom, her sister, and her sister's young son arrived yesterday. Liz's baby brother and his family came earlier today. I know that because they are on the committee. There might be more additions. I know that Rudolph is expecting some family members, and maybe other residents are too. I just hope that nobody is stuck in the storm. It sounds bad now, and it will get worse."

"What is the planning committee?" asked Sue, who overheard the conversation.

Clara handed her the phone.

"Uncle, what is the planning committee?"

"It is a committee for redesigning the vacant sites, previously set aside for the development of new homes, for raising crops and livestock to accommodate all the newcomers and make up for loss of providers of goods as a result of the upcoming natural disaster."

"I will be ready at nine. I am sure Mom will help me access the conference. For now, I have only one question. Why do we have to choose between more homes and more food? Isn't there a way to acquire more land and do both?"

"Good question, Sue. Until now, it has been impossible. The owners of the land surrounding us would not sell. I tried unsuccessfully to buy more land when I designed Oasis. But things may change. In the meantime, we need to work with what we have. Good night."

Sue was exhausted. She fell asleep oblivious to the thunderous cacophony created by the storm.

Clara could not sleep all night, being worried about Amalia and the children more than she was willing to admit to Sue. Early in the morning, she heard Stanly shrieking when he breathed.

"What is wrong?"

Stanly did not respond. Clara contacted Dr. Steve Grisham, who promised to do his best to reach them.

Steve fetched as much as medical equipment he could find and rushed into his trail car, a mini vehicle capable of traveling on the community-connecting roads. The shielding blanket was working, reducing the strength of the winds significantly, so travel within Oasis was possible. Clara was waiting for him and showed him to the bedroom once he arrived. Steve had seen many people die during the time he'd been in practice, but none of them had been an Oasis resident. A brief examination of Stanly suggested severe heart failure in need of immediate surgery, but to attempt to reach a hospital in this weather would be suicidal. He had no time to waste and needed to perform more tests.

"Clara, I will do the best I can without a hospital. If there is anything you can do, like send him healing energy or whatever healing practice is available to you, please do it. Also, keep talking to him."

Clara looked at him, terrified. She put her hands on Stanly's feet, sending him Reiki energy, and told him how much she loved him.

Steve hooked Stanly up to a multifunction monitor and an external pacemaker and prepared the IV therapy. He planned to insert into the IV a special tincture, his new invention for increasing blood flow into the atria while simultaneously augmenting the patient's stamina.

A knock on the door startled them. Nobody moved. They heard the door open, and then a young woman entered the room.

"Good morning. I am Chloe, Daphne's younger sister. I am a nurse. Daphne told me that you might need help."

"Hi, Chloe. I don't know why I did not think of calling you

myself. Do you know how to use the minilab? Can you help me analyze some blood samples?"

"Sure. Where is the minilab?"

She set the minilab on a small table in the corner while Steve drew some blood. While she was working on the analysis, Steve added two drops of his tincture into the IV liquid and murmured, "Please, God, make it work."

Until now, he had only experimented with the tincture in a simulator and on himself. It did work, based on his measurements, but he did not know what the right dose was or if it would help a person who was already experiencing heart failure. He watched the monitor and saw some alarming signals.

This is our last hope, he thought, adding more of his tincture. He was anxious and pale. Chloe showed him the results of the blood tests. The situation was worse than he'd thought. Clara noticed that Steve was about to break down. She moved close to Stanly's head, put her hands on his scalp, and visualized golden light penetrating his head and moving to his heart.

Steve was frantic, trying to figure out why the tincture had had no effect on Stanly. When he used it on himself, he had felt it immediately. In his despair, he called upon the mushroom that had appeared to him in his shamanic journey. And then he knew. Stanly's problem was also muscle weakness, which meant that Steve should add one of his other tinctures to the mixture. He found the tincture in his kit and inserted a few drops. The alarming red signals disappeared one by one, and Stanly opened his eyes.

A collective sigh of relief ensued. Chloe looked admiringly at Steve, who was still unable to grasp what had just happened.

"You did not have to journey for this one," said Clara, trying to diffuse the tension.

"You are wrong, Clara," responded Steve softly. "During my second journey at your home, I set the intention of finding a cure for heart failure. I did not receive dramatic instructions like when I needed a cure for the plague, but I did get some ideas, which I have experimented with since. In an ideal world, I would have tested my tincture more extensively before using it on a patient, but today I had no choice. It was the only thing I was aware of that could save him. Now I still want him to be checked into the hospital, weather permitting, but until then, he needs to rest a lot, eat healthy food, and avoid any stress, physical or mental."

Sue, who had just awakened, appeared ready for the teleconference. She was dumbfounded to see all the people around.

James Callahan walked in without knocking. "How is Stanly? Just heard the news from Daphne."

"Much better. Most certainly much better."

CHAPTER 18

HAVOC

The last three days had been some of the most traumatic to date in written history. The disasters that happened three years earlier, although devastating, dwarfed in comparison. An unusual heat wave precipitated the melting of the icecaps at both poles of the earth, and consequently the sea level rose six meters almost overnight. Many levees and seawalls were either too weak or not high enough to stop the gushing water. Many islands that had survived the continual rising waters and previous storms disappeared in a matter of hours. The coastal cities were the hardest hit, but the pouring rain, tornadoes, and heavy storms created flooding, mudslides, and destruction of unimaginable magnitude inland as well. Communication networks were damaged or obstructed, so it took about two weeks before anyone realized the magnitude of the death toll or the scope of the damage across the world, or even within the country. And the loss was beyond imagination. Governing institutions, weakened by prior disasters, collapsed and were not able to deal with burying the dead comforting the wounded, or protecting this new wave of homeless and destitute. The future was in the hands of the survivors.

Oasis had fared well, although Rudolph lost contact with his sister's family who were on their way to Oasis but weren't able to make it there in time. He knew what this meant and was not capable of sharing the community's joyful relief that the worst was over. He had a bitter feeling that everybody was happy and nobody cared about his family.

Oasis residents were capable of continuing their day-to-day activities within the boundaries of the community. The planning committee had made its recommendation to transform the six unassigned lots owned by the community into an agricultural food-producing area. Sustainit worked on designing and producing the appropriate greenhouses. Sue and Steve planned the allocation of crops to the various greenhouses and the appropriate soil, fertilization, temperature, and watering plan for each. Liz, with the help of Fred, tried to locate people who could sell more livestock, no small feat amid the mayhem. The school had successfully absorbed the new children. All were thankful to be living in Oasis and celebrated this fact in every meeting and at every communal meal.

And then the news from afar started coming in. Amalia finally succeeded in contacting her mother and related that she and her family were fine. After verifying that Sue had reached Oasis safely, she described in a shocked voice the hurricane that had hit their area. The city of Boston was flooded, as were many others cities on the East Coast. Thousands of people were dead, millions were injured or lacking food and clean water, and the magnitude of the damage to property was not yet known. Judging by the number of families made homeless overnight, it was enormous.

"Thank God Sue and the children left," Amalia said. "She certainly got the best end of the separation agreement. Their home was severely damaged, and both Josh and his lover were hospitalized with serious injuries. Several of the Geek Clique members were injured as well. Apparently, not every resident of the Callahan-built community followed the protective screen maintenance directives to the letter, which explains why several of them malfunctioned during the storm.

"Just to let you know, the elections took place a day before the hurricane hit, and I did win the seat in the Massachusetts House of Representatives, as you all predicted. Some elected members of our state congress are dead or wounded, and many of the surviving members are traumatized and incapable of dealing with the situation effectively. Anyway, I am a member of the disaster management task force, along with a few other capable people who can still think clearly. We have plenty of work. We are collaborating with the survivors in the Departments of Housing and Community Development, Health and Human Services, and Telecommunications. We are contacting counties and big cities to assess both the damage and their ability to cope and to ask what help they need. I suggested an ambitious plan to produce protective screens for each existing home, and to include them as required features in any new home, but I am not sure how to deal with the failures we just had. I would like to speak with James as soon as possible."

Clara, proud of her youngest daughter, contacted Callahan at once. Hearing about the failure of the protective screens and the damage in Prosperity, he appeared immediately and asked Amalia many questions about maintenance, availability of spare parts, and the current condition of the community. SCD had ceased to exist after his escape from East, and James did not know the whereabouts of his former employees. But he gave Amalia a few names of capable people from SCD and some names of companies he had strategic alliances with, and then he suggested that she try to locate these people and hire them for the job. He also gave her names of reliable companies that manufacture building materials and spare parts that she could contact. Callahan assured Amalia that he would always be available to provide distance counseling.

Callahan was very concerned about the malfunctioning of the protective screens. The nine communities he built were his babies, and he took their shortcomings personally, as a parent would, asking himself what he had done wrong in the raising of his children. Until this last calamity, all of them had withstood the natural disasters. He started calling the seven other communities and was terrified to find out that Sanctuary and Serenity suffered severe damage. Charisma in South California sustained some damage as well.

James summoned Sustainit engineers to an emergency meeting. It was crucial to determine if the cause of the equipment failure was negligence, inability to obtain spare parts, or equipment obsolescence. The engineers stated unanimously that the only reason for failure could be improper maintenance, adding that maintenance might be problematic in the absence of experts, spare parts, and enforcement of the necessary procedures. They all went to work checking Oasis's shielding blanket and making sure that the protective screens of each unit were operating properly. They reassured James that Oasis was safe.

That evening everyone gathered at the community center to listen to Governor Adam Hickman's speech. The big screen displayed a large picture of Governor Hickman, who looked quite dejected, a far cry from the enthusiastic and motivational figure that appeared on their home screen before. Hickman admitted his failure to ensure that all Colorado residents were safe, albeit Colorado was not one of the states hardest hit by the storms, thanks in large part to the work that had been done to better prepare homes to withstand natural catastrophes. He announced that he was planning to step down and suggested that the state congress plan for a new election as soon as possible.

It seemed that after dropping this bombshell, he felt somewhat better and started discussing what he was going to do until the upcoming elections. His efforts were going to focus on working with counties and cities, because in an emergency, only the closest people are capable of providing help. He suggested that local administrations conduct safety inspections of all existing usable homes and estimate the cost of better preparing them for future calamities. The state, he said, could provide guidelines and coordinate the inspections, but its budget was limited. "Local ingenuity is our most valuable treasure," he exclaimed. The governor also informed those present that his administration was preparing a list of contractors who were licensed to repair damaged properties and install safety features. Additionally, he was going to ask the state congress to approve an addition to the International Building Code to include mandatory basic safety features currently developed by the Office of the State Architect. Finally, he disclosed that the current interim president of the United States, Norris Gunderson, a survivor of the governing body appointed by the OD, was going to summon all the states' governors to discuss the future of the federation and the conduction of national elections. "I will be there," he added. He concluded by reiterating the need to work collaboratively and help each other and the community.

James was terrified. He looked at the faces of his comrades, and all he could see was fear. *People needed a motivational speech that expresses hope in the future, not to see their governor collapsing,* he thought. He had known Adam for many years and had never seen him so depressed. His thoughts raced. The two men were not close enough that James felt comfortable to call Adam on the phone. Something needed to be done, or the state would fall into chaos.

And then another speaker appeared on the screen, whom James identified as Jeff Platt, president of the Senate. Platt apologized for his unplanned appearance, stating that after having read the governor's intended speech, he knew he must follow him. Adding that the Senate expressed its unanimous support for the governor, Platt implored Governor Hickman to stay in office until the date of the scheduled elections. Platt argued that the state was not ready for early elections and said that the most urgent objectives were restoring life to normal as fast as possible and devising strategies for better coping with future disasters. "Adam Hickman, you are the right man for the job! Please don't attempt to dodge your responsibility," he declared.

James noticed that most people in the community center who were listening nodded in agreement. Governor Hickman appeared again, visibly moved, and thanked the Congress and the people of Colorado for trusting him. He vowed to do everything in his power to better prepare the state for future disasters.

The following day, Callahan sat in his Sustainit office and pondered possible ways he could support the survival endeavor. He started toying with the idea of reviving SCD, his old company, but he knew very well that this time around he should not create a new business but work with Sustainit. A phone call startled him and brought him back to reality.

"Hello, James. It is Adam Hickman. We have an enormous job ahead of us, and I need your help. I heard that you work for Sustainit now, which is great. I acknowledge that Sustainit helped to transform many residencies into storm-resistant properties that survived our last disaster. But we need to do much more, and fast. I would like you to lead Sustainit to play a greater role."

"Good to hear from you, Adam! First, let me express my and my neighbors' gratitude that you are our governor. We all trust you. Second, as you know, I am not Sustainit's owner, but I can speak with Mark and Donna. Any suggestions?"

"I would like to nominate Sustainit to be put in charge of helping all local administrations from Oasis east up to the Kansas border, and south all the way to the New Mexico border. It will not enrich Sustainit, but we will use state and local funds to cover the expenses.

Let me know if you have difficulty obtaining the materials or the workforce you need. Please contact me as soon as you discuss it with management."

Callahan stepped out of his office and met Mark, who invited him to an emergency staff meeting. Mark opened the meeting by posing the question of Sustainit's role in supporting the state endeavor. Callahan relayed the governor's request.

"James, please inform the governor that we are in. Evidently, this is not a request we can turn down. Both I and Donna believe that you are the right person to be in charge of doing the job. We will continue being in charge of design, innovation, and production. You will supervise the construction, manage the contacts with suppliers and the state and local administrations, and hire capable people. Speaking of inventions, I think we need to introduce our new extended weather shield. Each electronically charged weather shield can protect an area of about ten square miles and direct potential storms to travel high above the populated areas. Simultaneously, we will need to work on methods to avert potential nuclear fallout contamination. We do not believe that this danger is over yet. Do you accept the job?"

"Thanks for your trust, Mark. I do, and I will notify the governor at once! I know that applying your invention can save many lives in zones with many buildings that are not sufficiently protected, as there is not much we can do within a short period to protect individual buildings. Luckily, Colorado had a good database of the status of the buildings in each county before the last storms, and judging from Hickman's speech, they are going to update it as soon as possible. So we can start planning and prioritizing right away. I will see if I can get support for air purification given the enormous cost of restoring air quality after a major air-contamination event.

"But first, I need to carry out my responsibility as chair of Oasis's planning committee. We have to install our new greenhouses at home, prepare for planting and seeding, and finish the planting at home before we can help anybody else. I am going to deal with these things right away," he said. Then he left the office.

"Stanly! We need to summon everybody for a day of community work to get the new greenhouses in place," he said, having entered the home without knocking. Looking around for Stanly, he found him on his favorite couch on the balcony, facing a small bed of flowers, the only nonedible plants on the property. Stanly smiled faintly. "I am not feeling well. Why don't you do it yourself and ask Rudolph to conduct an election for a new president?"

"Will do. I hope you feel better soon."

James found Clara in the greenhouse and inquired about Stanly's condition. She asked Daphne to let Steve know as soon as he returned from the hospital. Since there was nothing she could do, she was keeping herself busy, trying to chase away her worries. She reiterated Stanly's request to be relieved of his duties.

James left. Calling Steve at once, he left a message. Next, he contacted Rudolph and asked him to arrange a community meeting this Wednesday evening and announce a community work day and potluck to take place on the upcoming Saturday.

Steve showed up early in the afternoon and offered to drive Stanly to the hospital. Stanly refused.

"If my time has come, I would rather die in my bed close to my family. The hospitals are crowded, and the treatment I would get there is riskier than staying at home."

"Stanly, all I can do is give you my tincture. It might strengthen you, but it will not cure you. You need to undergo thorough testing and probably surgery, neither of which can be done here. I can arrange a room for you."

"And I will be with you," added Clara.

"Dad, please go with Steve. We need you around here," whispered Sue, who had returned from Faithville after word about her father reached her.

"I know you all love me and wish me well. I also know that if sedated, I will not wake up. Steve, please do what you can. Leave the rest to God."

"Drink that," said Steve. "That's all I can do for you. I must return to the hospital. I will see you when I come back."

———————— ◆◆◆◆◆ ————————

On Wednesday morning, before the community meeting scheduled for the evening, James decided to visit Sanctuary, the first stop in his mission to increase safety and sustainability in the area. Although he had been troubled by the horror stories about the place and wanted to see the situation with his own eyes, he hoped that the recent destruction would convince the residents to collaborate in order to resolve their issues. This would enable him to turn the community into what he had dreamed it would become—a sanctuary.

So, he announced his visit to Sanctuary in his capacity as the governor's appointee for improving safety and sustainability. He was horrified to find that the community could not even decide who was going to meet him, as they had no governing body. He went anyway and started interviewing anybody who was willing to talk. There were only a few people willing, and those who did agree to report said they would only do so on one condition: anonymity.

The picture was grim. Sanctuary would never be able to emerge as a viable community because Jim's gang of five had foiled any genuine attempt to develop something positive. Callahan had a chance to make only a few home visits before Jim showed up and threatened him at gunpoint, telling him to leave the place. James had heard from Steve the story of his trip to Sanctuary to rescue Charlotte from Jim, who had threatened to kill her if she did not sleep with him, but he had dismissed it as Charlotte's issue. Now he got the picture. He turned around and hopped into his car. After Callahan left, Jim drove away from Sanctuary at maximum speed, barely missing a bullet meant for him, and disappeared into the horizon.

On his way back to Oasis, Callahan received a phone call telling him about Jim's escape and begging him to come back to Sanctuary and help. He did go back. He asked all the residents to convene in the community center, which looked impressive, situated on a small hill in the middle of the village. Callahan was the first to enter the center. Immediately he ran out in horror. "This place is worse than a pigpen!" he exclaimed. "If you want to receive any assistance, you should clean it up now."

Douglas Morrison, the former financier, suggested that they meet at somebody's home and elect a council or at least a president.

"What happened to the one you elected two years ago?" asked Callahan.

"Some people from Jim's gang fabricated evidence that Albert Morell was spying for the Order Defenders. As a result, he was arrested," responded Bob, who was a member of the gang. "We had no choice. He would have killed my wife and children if I did not comply. I wish I hadn't missed the shot. I hope you will make sure he will never return, Mr. Callahan."

"Why did you wait so long?"

"He made sure that the gang members did not trust each other. He promised a big reward to whoever informed him of another gang member's betrayal, and he guaranteed that horrible consequences would befall these traitors."

"Would you repeat what you have just told me if asked by the governor or summonsed to court?"

"I will if you guarantee summonsed protection for my family and me."

Callahan called the governor using the emergency hotline.

"I am in an important meeting. Is the matter really urgent?"

"It is. I am in Sanctuary. Jim Carver, a man everybody fears, has escaped. Consequently, I heard an interesting confession. I would like you to listen to the testimony and then free Albert Morrel, who was the president of Sanctuary and was falsely detained. Also, I would like you to do your best to arrest Jim, as he might return and take revenge."

"Bob, will you please tell Governor Hickman what you have just said to me?"

A trembling Bob picked up the phone and told Governor Hickman that Jim had planted a phone in Albert Morrell's home with recordings of fake conversations between him and the OD, and some false documents as well.

"James, Cleve Summers, the general attorney, here. I heard the testimony and recorded it. Please send me electronically an affidavit signed by the rest of the gang. I will free the man as soon as I receive it."

Callahan made clear to the rest of the gang that they had better sign or else. The other three men were visibly upset but knew they had no choice but to comply if they wanted to have any chance of coming out clean. Callahan sent the affidavit. Later that evening, Albert Morrison was home.

Callahan, knowing that Sanctuary was not the only community plagued by internal terrorism, decided to bring it up at the next meeting with the governor and the Safety and Sustainability Commission. He was very aware that Sanctuary's problems were not over.

CHAPTER 19

HOPE

The mood was grim at the community center when Callahan entered. He noticed the absence of Stanly, Clara, Sue, and Steve. All were saddened by the task of electing a new president, but they acknowledged that it was necessary. Rudolph nominated James, who, after expressing his appreciation, declined the nomination, stating that his new responsibilities would probably involve travel and saying that the president should be someone who works in Oasis and can respond quickly in case of emergency.

"I nominate you," James added.

"I am already the coordinator of communications," responded Rudolph. "I suggest that we elect somebody who is not already on the village council. I nominate Ralph, our banker."

"And I nominate Dave, our innovative genius engineer," said Donna.

Rudolph counted the votes and declared Ralph as the new Oasis Council president. As Rudolph was getting ready to adjourn the meeting, Steve entered the room.

"I am glad you are still here. I have just seen Stanly. There is no change in his condition. I think that we need to allocate some space in the community center for a clinic. I will keep visiting sick people in their homes, but some procedures require the use of heavy equipment and more space. I cannot do it in my home, as I no longer have room for it," he said, smiling shyly at Daphne, whose due date was near. I have a minilab that can perform many tests, a simple screener, and a robotic surgeon. I need at least one room for equipment and treatment and another for the lab and office space for me and Chloe, who did a fantastic job assisting me with Stanly."

"Can you perform surgeries here?" asked a surprised Freda, uttering a question that seemed to be on other people's minds as well.

"I am not a surgeon or an anesthesiologist, but with the help of the robotic surgeon I can perform simple surgeries requiring only local sedation."

"I think Steve is right. We need a clinic. Why don't you use one of the community center's second-floor apartments? All three are vacant now," said Vanessa.

"Unfortunately, we have no elevator, and very sick people would not be able to climb to the second floor. The clinic has to be easily accessible and on the first floor," responded Steve.

"It can be done," replied Henri. We can turn the two rooms behind the kitchen into a clinic. They are large, just to the right of the entrance to the center. I will be able to add a small washroom as well. I will draw up the designs and check with you before remodeling."

"How long will it take?" asked Steve, visibly anxious.

"I will show you the plan tomorrow, and if it is approved, I can get it done within a week. I hope we will not have any surprises." He chuckled, looking at Daphne.

"We will use an apartment on the second floor for our junior and high school kids. They would love to have some privacy and could use some exercise," said Laura.

◆◆◆◆◆◆◆

Steve's tension grew as Daphne's due date approached. He hoped she would be able to give birth in the hospital so that if she needed a C-section or encountered other complications, there would be professional physicians and nurses to take care of her. But in his dreams, he saw himself performing surgery using the robotic surgeon.

For years he'd studied the procedures of certain operations, knowing quite well that in an emergency situation, he might be the only one available to perform these surgeries. He'd watched many operations and even performed some when there was a shortage of surgeons. He even performed a C-section surgery once. But it was in the hospital, with the help of nurses and other professional staff, and the patient was not his wife.

He was a frugal person but had pinched pennies to purchase the best medical equipment available on the market, including the most sophisticated robotic surgeon, so he would be ready to help Oasis residents, and possibly others, when going to Faithville was too dangerous or when the patient needed immediate attention. So far, he had not used it.

The fact that Stanly's condition was frail and he would not go to the hospital added to Steve's growing anxiety. Stanly was his first Oasis patient with a life-threatening condition. Without a thorough battery of tests done in the hospital, he could not determine what should be done to assist his heart functioning. He knew very well that his tinctures would not sustain Stanly for very long, and neither would Clara's Reiki or the other procedures she had been using. The only heartening fact was that Henri applied himself to the creation of a clinic with zeal. Steve planned to move his expensive equipment there soon.

Oasis had not had many visitors recently, especially not in the evening time. So, when a motor home entered Oasis Road and circled the community center, heading toward the Steiners' home, people went out to see who was coming. Amalia, her husband, Dave, and their children, Evie and Saul, emerged from the vehicle and entered the house without noticing the curious and concerned looks of the neighbors. Amalia had taken a short leave from her urgent work in Massachusetts after hearing about her father's condition. Callahan showed up, as always willing to help, and offered to host Amalia and her family. They preferred to stay in their vehicle for now, to be closer to the family. Clara and Sue invited all of them to eat a hearty dinner. A very pale and visibly frail Stanly smiled and chatted happily with the grandchildren he had not seen for a few years. The four children were frolicking. The adults attempted to conceal their deep worry. Amalia, intending to get Callahan's attention and receive as much information as possible for her work in Massachusetts, could not ignore the way he looked at her beautiful older sister. Neither could Clara. The two exchanged an understanding look.

Unrelenting Amalia did succeed in having a conversation with Callahan about his favorite topic, sustainability. Callahan promised Amalia that he would provide her with the details of the new weather shield and suggested the idea that the Geek Clique or some other Eastern nerd group would found a startup to produce and install protection shields in Massachusetts and beyond.

On the following morning, a beautiful and peaceful Saturday, Steve, helped by Henri and Chloe, moved the medical equipment to the new clinic and borrowed some of the center's furniture for the office and small waiting room. Daphne brought some of her pictures. Steve and Henri hung two portraying peaceful lakeside landscapes in the treatment room, and the two more dramatic ones in the office and lab chamber. Henri proudly hung a big sign on the door that read, Oasis Clinic. "We are ready," he declared. Steve thanked him warmly.

"Don't thank me, brother; you never know who will need it or when!"

Steve went to the Steiners' home to invite Stanly to be the first patient. When nobody answered his knocking, he opened the door hesitantly. *Am I too late?* he wondered. Hearing some murmurs from the bedroom area, he headed over. Stanly was lying in bed, surrounded by his wife, his two daughters, his grandchildren, and James, all expressing their love and appreciation of him. He was at peace and ready to go. He then noticed Steve at the corner of the room.

"Thank you, Doctor. Without your tinctures, I would not have lived to say goodbye to all my beloved. I love you all. Being Oasis's first president was my greatest honor. I want to be buried here in Oasis. Clara, the love of my life, I hope you will find the energy to conduct the ceremony. It need not follow the religious protocol, as long as somebody, probably Sue, says the Kaddish." He breathed wearily. Everybody held their breath.

James was staying with Clara and Sue. The familiar face of Rudolph appeared on everybody's screen.

"Good evening to you. I am sorry to announce that Stanly Steiner, our first president, died this afternoon, surrounded by family and friends. The funeral will take place tomorrow at 2:00 p.m. Oasis Council decided in an emergency meeting to designate half of unit 18 at the northwestern corner of Oasis as a cemetery. The family asks that you respect their privacy until the funeral. Everyone is welcome to read a short eulogy or literary piece at the ceremony and visit the family afterward."

On the following day, Jacob and his girlfriend arrived from Faithville, and Edna, Clara's sister, and her family came from Refuge. Jacob succeeded in reaching his mother in California. Just before the ceremony, a sobbing Sophie called and asked to be a part of it somehow. Jacob promised to telemovie the ceremony to her. She mentioned that she had given birth to a baby girl who was now two months old, saying that the child and her family were doing fine.

They all gathered at the designated place on time. James and Jacob Callahan, Rudolph, Steve, Mark, and Dave carried the coffin that Fred had somehow obtained. The family followed them to the dedicated lot, and they all stood around the open grave. The men lowered the coffin into the grave while Clara, wearing a long black and white gown, trying to overcome her emotions, sang the prayer. Sue said the Kaddish, and then Clara, followed by all the family members, eulogized their beloved husband, father, and grandfather. The atmosphere was solemn. Ralph, the community banker and the newly elected president, delivered a eulogy on behalf of Oasis Council. Daphne read a poem. Judy played a short violin piece by Bach, and Laura expressed gratitude for Stanly's contribution to the school and his amazing rapport with his young students.

All felt that Oasis's first chapter had come to an end. They offered consolation to the bereaved family, sensing that they were mourning not only Stanly's death but also the end of Oasis's childhood innocence.

Amalia and her family were first to leave after hearing the forecast of a new storm approaching. Edna and her family followed suit. Jacob and his girlfriend returned to Faithfield after staying with James for a week. It seemed that life was slowly returning to normal.

Sue was glad to be at her mother's side during this trying time, and Clara found solace watching her two grandchildren.

Sue, who was on the cusp of discovering a new way of enriching the soil for improving greenhouse yields, could not wait to return to her lab at Faithfield State. As oblivious to her surroundings as she was, she could not ignore the fact that James had started showing an increased interest in her work, and could not disregard his underlying intentions. She had always liked her uncle James and admired his free and adventurous spirit and his inventiveness, but she considered him an uncle, not a potential lover. Still, although she was not yet ready for a new man in her life, she enjoyed his admiring looks, which helped to heal the wounds Josh's betrayal had left in her heart. Occasionally, she smiled at him as a woman, not as a niece admiring her uncle.

Callahan instructed Sustainit to prioritize their support so that they could help as many as families as possible in a short time. The idea was to encourage communities to draft their residents to help with the construction and repair, as Sustainit, concentrating on massive production, could not hire enough people to install the sustainability and safety products. As Callahan anticipated, when communities succeeded in organizing for the project, this increased communal cohesion. But to his chagrin, he found that even the threat of an upcoming disaster and the promise of help did not suffice to move many of the dysfunctional communities forward. Callahan also made sure to protect greenhouses, stores of food and other goods, and factories. In spite of all the difficulties, the progress made by Callahan, Sustainit, and the collaborating builders was quite impressive.

James listened to the dreaded alarm when he was eating supper at his kitchen after a long day at Sustainit. The communications system broadcasted Rudolph's announcement of approaching weather turbulence that would involve very severe storms, a few tornadoes, and torrential rain. Rudolph expected it would last about three days and suggested that nobody leave Oasis during that period. James knew that by now, people were used to the drill and knew how to prepare. His greatest fear was that although up to now Oasis had been spared from all the disasters thanks to his and others' sophisticated inventions and dedicated maintenance work, there was always the possibility that something would malfunction. Sustainit engineers' contention that system malfunctions in other communities were due to mere poor maintenance were unconvincing. He closed his safety shutters as he watched a wild, menacing bolt of lightning and heard the rolling thunder. Then he made a mental note of all the machinery located at Sustainit. Trusting nobody, he had checked everything himself before the storm hit.

All of a sudden his internal-communication device buzzed and blinked. It was a message from Mark. "James, something is wrong with the weather-controlling device. I hear a terrible noise. I need your help diagnosing and hopefully fixing the problem. Be careful. Go right to the factory."

James knew what this meant. There was a good chance that Oasis would fall victim to the type of destruction that had befallen some of his other communities. "On my way," he replied. He put on his storm suit, waited for the hurricane-force gust to subside some, and ran as fast as he could. Entering the building, he heard a shrieking noise. Mark was waiting for him, looking at the instruments. "I have checked out the function of every piece," Mark said.

"I think one of the turbines is giving up. I will have our robot carry up some replacement parts. When I give you the signal, stop the machine. I will let you know when to restart it," James said.

"Be careful, James," said Mark. James was on his way up as Mark continued working on the diagnostics. James identified the source of the noise, gave instructions to the robot, and accompanied it to the roof to make sure that all was done properly and that the robot could perform in the gusty wind. He tied himself with chains to two poles to make sure the wind would not blow him too far. Then he instructed Mark to stop the machines. When nothing moved, he instructed the robot to start. He was watching the robot, holding strong against the wind and the heavy rain, almost deafened by the thunder. He was in his element, determined and smiling. *We are going to make it,* he thought. *Almost done.* Then a strong gust threw him off balance, and he hit the pole. It hurt, but he knew that nothing was broken. The robot had been tossed about as well and looked damaged. James completed the final steps.

"Are you okay?" messaged Mark.

"I am, but the robot is dead. Please restart the machines. I want to make sure everything works properly."

"Perfecto," messaged Mark. "All the diagnostics are A-OK. Come down, buddy."

That night, Daphne awoke at one point and told Steve softly, "Darling, I think our baby is coming. I tried to hang on and let you sleep, but the time has come." Steve jumped out of bed, hugged his beloved wife, and notified Chloe to come to the clinic. He held Daphne tight and, fighting the blowing winds, arrived at the clinic and set up the equipment as he had rehearsed many times. Chloe and Nina showed up, and unexpectedly Clara appeared, uttering that she'd seen the lights on in the clinic and thought they might need help. Steve set the screener to get a picture of the status of the baby. The diagnosis was that given the baby's position, emergency surgery was required at once.

"Don't worry, Daphne. Everything will be okay," he uttered, administering the local sedative.

"I am not worried, dear, I trust you."

"We all believe in you, Steve," said Clara, sensing that he was the one who needed reassurance at that point. She tapped his shoulder lightly, and all of a sudden he became very calm. He was thankful that she was around. He set up the surgical robot and started the operation.

Half an hour later he heard a baby cry. Clara and Nina washed the baby and placed it at Daphne's side while Steve was completing the surgery. "It's a girl!" said Nina.

"All done," said Steve. "How do you feel, my love?"

"Couldn't be happier or more proud."

Clara handed the cleaned and bundled-up baby to Steve, who, teary-eyed and relieved, held his new daughter.

Suddenly they saw James, dripping wet in his storm suit, coming in.

"I was just changing a broken turbine," he said, holding his head and almost falling into an empty chair. Steve handed the baby to

Daphne and ran to James. He took off his helmet. James's head was bleeding, and he looked delirious. Steve asked Chloe to bandage James's head while he examined him and performed some tests. He connected some electrodes to James's scalp and looked at his screen.

"Looks like a mild concussion. He will be okay, but he should rest. He should not be home alone, though."

"Steve, he is running a high temperature, 103° F to be accurate," said Chloe.

"I felt it and have already given him something to reduce his temperature."

"Sue," whispered James. Clara smiled. "Steve, can you help me take him to our place? We will take good care of him."

"Sure," he said. "We will place him in the trail car. Don't hesitate to call me if something goes wrong."

"I will be right back." He smiled to Daphne.

Clara turned to Daphne.

"What are you going to name our first Oasis-born baby?" All eyes looked at Daphne.

"Hope," she said. "Her name is Hope."

Printed in the United States
By Bookmasters